"I presume I'm allowed to do this much for you?" Nacho said, opening the door.

Did she appear so prickly and defensive? Probably, Grace concluded. She wasn't cut out for the role of victim, but there was no reason to overreact to every little comment, either. Feeling for the seat, she climbed into the car and Nacho swung into the driver's seat at her side.

It was when he closed the door and they were trapped inside the small space together that information started bombarding her brain. He was still damp from the shower. He had used some sort of menthol soap—or was that toothpaste? Or mouthwash, maybe? Anyway, he smelled clean. Big and warm was a given, as was bursting with suppressed energy. She held herself stiffly as he started the engine—sensing his hands close, but unable to tell just how close.

Tension was rising all the time between them—or maybe she was imagining that, too. She wondered if, at the thought of the test to come, Nacho's lips were twisted in the cynical smile she remembered.

SUSAN STEPHENS was a professional singer before meeting her husband on the tiny Mediterranean island of Malta. In true Harlequin Presents style, they met on Monday, became engaged on Friday and were married three months later. Almost thirty years and three children later, they are still in love. (Susan does not advise her children to return home one day with a similar story, as she may not take the news with the same fortitude as her own mother!)

Susan had written several nonfiction books when fate took a hand. At a charity costume ball there was an after-dinner auction. One of the lots, "Spend a Day with an Author," had been donated by Harlequin Presents author Penny Jordan. Susan's husband bought this lot and Penny was to become not just a great friend, but a wonderful mentor who encouraged Susan to write romance.

Susan loves her family, her pets, her friends and her writing. She enjoys entertaining, travel and going to the theater. She reads, cooks and plays the piano to relax, and can occasionally be found throwing herself off mountains on a pair of skis or galloping through the countryside.

Visit Susan's website, www.susanstephens.net. She loves to hear from her readers all around the world!

Other titles by Susan Stephens available in ebook:

Harlequin Presents® Extra

183—WORKING WITH THE ENEMY

Harlequin Presents

3009—THE UNTAMED ARGENTINIAN

3058—THE ARGENTINIAN'S SOLACE*

*linked to A TASTE OF THE UNTAMED

To find out more about the wild Acosta family visit:

http://www.susanstephens.com/acostas/index.html

ED

A TASTE OF
THE UNTAMED

SUSAN STEPHENS

~ Dark, Demanding and Delicious ~

HARLEQUIN®
entertain, enrich, inspire™

ISBN-13: 978-0-373-52893-6

A TASTE OF THE UNTAMED

Copyright © 2012 by Susan Stephens

www.Harlequin.com

Printed in U.S.A.

A TASTE OF
THE UNTAMED

For Penny

CHAPTER ONE

'NACHO Acosta is back in circulation!'

Screwing up her eyes as she stared at the screen, Grace blinked and tried to clear her vision. The virus she had contracted must be affecting her eyesight, she concluded, reading on: *'Romily Winner, our Up-Town sleuth, reports on the trail of who's hot and who's not.'*

Oh, damn…

Now there were white spots dancing in front of her eyes and the monitor screen was flashing. Pushing her chair back, Grace stood to stretch her aching limbs and inhale a lungful of stale basement air. She squeezed her eyes shut again and then blinked several times.

Better.

Relieved to find the problem had cleared, she checked the PC connections.

All good.

Tiredness, Grace concluded. It *was* almost one a.m. Working as a cocktail waitress in the half-light of a nightclub in Cornwall and then sitting in the club's office working on accounts for half the night was hardly going to make for happy eyes.

Tired or not, Grace made one last trawl over the countless images of aggressively handsome men featured on the society pages of *ROCK!* magazine, finding it hard to believe that she had met the infamous Nacho Acosta in the hard, tanned flesh. They could hardly be said to inhabit the same world, but fate played funny tricks sometimes.

Finally managing to drag her gaze away from the photographs of Nacho, she got on with devouring every word the journalist had written about him...

With the wild Acostas all grown up and fully fledged, this reporter doubts that Nacho—at thirty-two the oldest of the notorious polo-playing Acosta brothers—will be in much hurry to quit the London scene, where he seems to be finding plenty to keep him entertained!

Grace felt a pulse of arousal even as her stomach clenched with jealousy at the thought of all the other women *entertaining* Nacho, as the reporter so suggestively put it. Which was ridiculous, bearing in mind she'd only met him twice, and on each occasion had felt so clumsy and awkward in comparison to Nacho's effortless style she hardly had any right to feel so much as a twinge of envy.

But she did.

The first time they had met had been at a polo match on the beach in Cornwall, which Grace's best friend and Nacho's sister, Lucia, had arranged. Nacho had done little more on that occasion than lean out of the window of his monster Jeep to give Grace a quick once-over, but no man had ever looked at her that way before, and she could still remember the effect on her body of so much heat. She'd spent the rest of the day watching Nacho playing polo from the sidelines like some lovesick teenager.

They had met for a second time at Lucia's wedding,

held at the Acosta family's main *estancia* in Argentina. This trip had been the greatest thrill of Grace's life— until she'd seen Nacho in the giant marquee and his keen black stare had found her. He'd been tied up for most of the evening, hosting the event, but she had felt the effect of his powerful charisma wherever she went, so that by the time he'd found a chance to speak to her she had only been able to stare at him like a fool, wide-eyed and stumped for words.

Growing up with parents who had extolled her virtues to anyone who would listen had left Grace with crippling shyness, for the simple reason that she knew she could never be as beautiful or as gifted as they made her out to be. A lot of that shyness had been knocked out of her at the club, where the patrons appreciated her efficiency, but it had all come flooding back that night at the wedding in front of Nacho, transforming what could have been a flirty, fun encounter into a tongue-tied mess.

Shifting her mind from that embarrassing occasion, Grace studied another shot of the man who'd once rocked her world. There was yet another beautiful woman at his side, and Grace had to admit they made a striking couple. And the girl's expression seemed to warn every other woman off.

'You can have him,' Grace muttered, dragging her gaze away. Nacho Acosta might be gorgeous, but that night at the wedding had proved he was well out of her league.

The sound of the nightclub pianist running through his repertoire provided a welcome distraction for Grace, who had always found company in music and books. Her parents had once had high hopes that Grace would become a concert pianist, but those dreams had ended when her father had died and there had been no more money to pay her fees at the *conservatoire*. Grace hadn't realised how cossetted she had been until that moment, or what loss really meant. Losing her place at college had been devastating, but losing her father had been far, far worse.

Leaving music college had forced Grace to find a job, and she had been grateful to find a position in a nightclub where one of the top jazz musicians of the day performed. Being close to music at that level had been a small comfort to Grace, who had still been suffering greatly from the death of her father.

Turning back to the computer screen again, Grace studied the picture at the end of the article showing Lucia and her brothers. Lucia was smiling, while each of her brothers either appeared dangerous, brooding or stern. Nacho was at the dangerous end of the spectrum.

It must have been hard for Lucia, Grace reflected. The only girl in a family of four men, how had Lucia ever made herself heard, or seen, or taken account of at all? Lucia had once mentioned that being alone in the Acosta family had never been an option. It was little wonder that she had made a bid for freedom, Grace mused, leaving the family home to work in the club where the two girls had met. Nacho had raised his siblings when their parents had been killed in a flood, and though Lucia was always upbeat by nature she referred to that time as like being under the heel of the tyrant.

Grace shivered involuntarily as she studied Nacho's face. Everyone knew Nacho Acosta to be a forceful man, who got everything he wanted.

'Piano-time, Grace?'

She turned at the sound of Clark Mayhew's voice as he poked his head around the door. Clark was the club pianist she so loved to hear.

'Come on, Grace,' Clark prompted. 'Shut that computer down and get out here. You've got a real talent.'

'Not like you,' she said, smiling.

Clark shrugged. 'The only difference between you and me is that I have more confidence.'

'I wish!' Grace exclaimed, laughing as she walked across the club, sat down and adjusted the piano stool. 'I can't even play without music like you. I only wish I could.'

'But you can,' Clark insisted. 'Close your eyes and let the melody flow through your fingers...'

A bolt of panic hit her as Grace realised she had no option but to close her eyes. The moment she tried to focus her eyes on the music notes and lines began to wheel and collide on the page.

'Close your eyes, Grace,' Clark encouraged, oblivious to what was happening. 'Didn't I tell you?' he said when she managed a few bars.

She would definitely have to cut down her screentime, Grace realised when she opened her eyes again. The flashing lights plaguing her vision hadn't gone away. If anything, they were getting worse.

Two years later

The girl had been eyeing him up since he'd entered the ballroom. It was a magnificent room, currently set out for a formal dinner with small tables laid for eight. An armada of glass and silverware glittered beneath huge Venetian chandeliers, which proved the perfect spotlight for the girl trying to attract his attention. Her figure alone was enough to scramble any man's head, and the heated invitation in her eyes promised only one conclusion—if he were interested.

He'd pass. He was restless tonight, and bored by the round of engagements his PA had set up for him in London.

Tonight was a so-called power dinner, for movers and shakers in the wine industry. Nacho was better known for playing polo at an international level and running an *estancia* in Argentina the size of a small country, but his decision to restore the family vineyards was something he had been forced to do in order to protect his siblings' inheritance. Nothing else would have persuaded him to return to that particular family home in Argentina...

'Nacho.'

He turned to see the dapper figure of Don Fernando Gonzales, the chairman of the event, approaching. 'Don Fernando.' He inclined his head politely, noting the sultry beauty was now standing at the chairman's side.

'Nacho Acosta—I would like to present my daughter, Annalisa Gonzales...'

As Don Fernando stepped back an all too familiar sensation came over him as he briefly clasped the woman's carefully manicured hand. He'd heard Don Fernando was in financial trouble, and the portly chairman wouldn't be the first father to parade his pretty daughter in front of Nacho. Everyone knew Nacho held the reins to the family fortune, though they seemed unaware that Nacho was wise to schemes born out of desperation, or that he could do more damage to those he cared about than those misguided parents could possibly imagine.

It was almost a relief when he was distracted by the glimpse of a shining blonde head. He stared across the room, trying to work out if he had met the blonde before. His sixth sense said yes, but with only the back of her head to go on it was hard to be sure...

'Am I keeping you, Señor Acosta?' Annalisa Gonzales asked him with a knowing look.

Her father had peeled away, Nacho noticed, giving them the chance to get to know each other better. 'Forgive me,' he said, forcing himself to concentrate on what was undeniably a beautifully designed face.

'Are you really as bad as they say you are?' Annalisa asked, as if she hoped it were true.

'Worse,' he assured her.

They were both distracted by the sound of a dog barking, and Annalisa laughed as she turned to look for the culprit. 'If I had known dogs were permitted at this dinner I would have brought Monkey, my Chihuahua—'

'Who would have provided a tasty snack for Cormac, my Irish Wolfhound,' he countered. 'If you will excuse me, Señorita Gonzales, I believe the MC is about to call us to our tables…'

Grace sat down, relieved to have the woman sitting next to her introduce herself right away. Elias, Grace's elderly employer and mentor, was sitting on Grace's other side, but he had been immediately swept into greeting old friends and colleagues, and Grace was keen to prove that she could do this by herself. This annual event in celebration of the wine industry was Grace's first major outing since becoming blind. It was also the first big outing for her guide dog, Buddy, and Grace was as nervous for Buddy as she was for herself. She hoped they would both get through the evening without making too many blunders.

While Grace was chatting easily to the lady at her side she took the chance to discreetly map the tablecloth and all the various hazards confronting her. A battalion of glasses was waiting to be knocked over—and then there was the cutlery she had to get right. And the napkin she had to unfold without knocking anything over. There were a lot of different-sized plates, along with groups of condiments and sugar bowls. The potential for sugar in her soup and salt in her coffee loomed large.

'Here's the pepper, if you want it,' the lady next to her remarked, flagging up the arrival of the soup. 'I like pepper on everything,' she added, 'though you may want to taste first. It might need salt—'

Grace felt a rush of emotion as the woman placed a second container close to her hand, where Grace could feel it. Small kindnesses counted for a lot now she was blind. They meant she could leave the house and do things like this. Elias was right. All she had to do was buckle on her courage each morning along with Buddy's harness. It was harder doing that sometimes than talking about it, but it helped to know there were some really nice people in the world—and thank goodness for them.

'You work for one of the great men in our industry,' the older woman commented, obviously impressed when Grace explained that Elias had trained her to be a sommelier.

'I guess Elias is the closest thing I've got to a father figure,' Grace admitted. It wasn't enough to describe Elias as her employer when he'd done so much for her.

'You lost your father?' the elderly lady prompted gently.

'Yes,' Grace murmured, growing sombre as she thought back.

'I lost my father when I was very young. You're lucky to have Elias on your side. He's a kind man and a good man, and there aren't many of those around—though I'm sure you'll meet a good man of your own one day and get married.'

'Oh, no!' Grace exclaimed. 'I could never do that.'

'Why ever not?' Grace's companion demanded as Buddy barked at the change in Grace's voice.

'I wouldn't want to be a burden,' Grace explained.

'A burden?' her new friend exclaimed. 'Whatever gave you that idea?'

Grace would run a mile rather than be a burden to anyone. She'd felt the same way when her mother had found happiness again after her father's death and had wanted to marry a man with children of his own. Grace hadn't wanted to get in the way of her mother's happiness, and had taken the marriage as her cue to leave home for good. Then, when her sight had deteriorated, she had become doubly determined not to be a trouble to anyone.

But she wasn't about to spoil this evening with dark thoughts. 'I've still got a lot to learn and a lot to get used to,' Grace said lightly, 'so I think perhaps I'd better get myself sorted out before I go looking for love,' She laughed, realizing what she'd said. 'Perhaps it would be better if I let love come looking for me.' She stilled, feeling a warm, papery hand covering hers.

'You're a brave girl, Grace. You deserve the best,' Grace's new friend insisted. 'And don't you dare settle for anything less.'

Nacho was growing increasingly impatient—although as Annalisa shrugged her slender shoulders and walked away he was forced to ask himself when the chance to accept a free gift in such attractive packaging had become so meaningless.

The past had made him hard and cynical, Nacho concluded. Most of the women he encountered seemed so obvious and shallow, and they all wanted the same thing:

someone—anyone—to take care of them, financially and emotionally. And, having spent his teens and twenties caring for his siblings, he found his emotional bank was drained.

His married brothers often talked of how lucky they were to have found a soul mate. He always laughed and asked what chance they thought he stood. If they answered him he never listened. He didn't believe in fate or luck. Hard work brought results, and he didn't have time to waste searching for a woman. The only woman who could possibly stir his interest now would have to be strong and independent.

He cast one last look around the room, searching for the blonde again, but she seemed to have gone. He could be doing better things with his time, and as soon as politeness allowed he made his excuses and left.

On the drive back to the family penthouse in London he couldn't shake the feeling that something of significance had happened at the dinner, though what that might have been eluded him.

Working in a vast wine warehouse was easy for Grace now she had Buddy to guide her. The big Golden Retriever could happily steer Grace across London, and navigating the now familiar maze of passages at the warehouse was a breeze for him, so Grace was curious when he started to growl.

'What's the matter, boy?' she said, bending low to give him a pat. The strange thing was she could feel something too. It was the same sense of foreboding she got when there was thunder in the air.

Since her sight had failed Grace had come to rely on her other senses, and they had quickly become more developed. But apart from the thundering of her heart she could hear nothing now. 'We've only got one more section to check,' she reassured her guide dog. 'Take me to Argentina, Buddy...'

Hearing one of his command words, Buddy led Grace unerringly to the section in the warehouse where wines from Argentina were stored. If Grace had said Spain, or France, or New World, the highly trained guide dog would have known exactly where to take her. To make doubly sure there could never be a mistake each section was labelled in Braille as well as in script.

Grace had had to learn a lot of new things since losing her sight to a rare virus. At first numbness and denial at the bleakness of her prognosis had swept over her, keeping her chained to the bed, to the house, but then anger and frustration had taken over, and they had demanded action. She'd decided that didn't want to spend the rest of her life blundering around and falling over things, and had finally determined she would learn to trust the hated stick.

'The Stick' had sat in a corner of Grace's bedroom since her return from hospital, where a therapist had assured her in no uncertain terms that if she didn't use it to get out of the house she would spend her life in darkness.

'But I *am* in darkness!' Grace had yelled in angry desperation.

There had been a lot of screaming and yelling as well as quiet sobbing through those dark, difficult times. It had changed nothing. Having Elias in the background, nagging her constantly to get on with her life, had worked, and finally picking up 'The Stick' had changed her life. It had been her first step towards independence.

But just when she had gathered enough courage to walk down the road she'd realized everything above waist-height slapped her in the face. On one outing she

had crept home, feeling her way an inch at a time…
like a blind woman. And another week had been wasted
grieving for what couldn't be changed. It was only when
Lucia had turned up with a representative from the Guide
Dogs' Association that Grace had been persuaded to try
something new.

At first she had protested that she couldn't look after
herself, never mind a dog, but to her shock Lucia had
snapped angrily, 'For goodness' sake, pull yourself together, Grace. Buddy needs feeding—and he needs regular walks. This isn't all about *you,* Grace.'

Grace had slowly realized that she had been behaving incredibly selfishly and had immersed herself in a
lonely world of her own making. She had given Lucia
every cause to be worried about her progressively with-
drawn friend.

When Buddy had arrived everything had changed.
From the moment the big dog snuggled up to Grace it
was a done deal. Buddy alerted her to every hazard, and
by doing so opened up Grace's world. Lucia, as usual,
had gone overboard, enthusing and saying that as Buddy
was already chipped and inoculated, and had his very
own doggy passport, there was no excuse for Grace not
to go travelling.

As if! Grace had thought at the time. Though now,
thanks to Buddy, her confidence was building daily.

'What *is* your problem?' Grace demanded fondly as
Buddy continued to growl. She relaxed when she heard
the voice of her mentor, Elias Silver. Elias had used to
supply the club with wine, which was how they'd met,
and he'd offered her a job when no one else would, en-
couraging Grace to retrain as sommelier. 'Elias must be
meeting someone,' she commented, stroking Buddy's

silky ears. 'You'll have to get used to people you don't know now we're both working full-time.'

Grace had barely returned to her office when Elias came in, full of suppressed excitement.

'The new wines I've just been tasting are exceptional.'

'And?' Grace prompted, sensing there was more to come.

She grew increasingly uneasy as the silence lengthened.

'I've known about this vineyard for years,' Elias started telling her, in a tone that suggested he was choosing his words carefully. 'I was planning for us to go to Argentina together, Grace—'

She did a mental double-take. This was the first she'd heard of it.

Argentina—so far away. And impossible for her to visit now she was blind.

Argentina—the home of the Acostas and Nacho—

'Don't look so shocked,' Elias insisted. 'You know I've been slowing down recently...'

Grace's thoughts whirled. Elias being less than fit was a terrifying prospect. He was a dear friend.

'You'll have to go to Argentina without me,' he said.

'Sorry?' she breathed in a shocked voice.

'If there was any alternative, believe me, I would suggest it, Grace, but my doctor has insisted I must rest.'

'Then you *must* rest, and I'll look after you,' Grace insisted.

'The business can't afford for both of us to be away at the same time, and I'm not going to risk losing out on top-quality wine to a competitor. You have to go, Grace. Who else can I ask? Who else can I trust?'

'But what if I let you down?'

'You won't,' Elias assured her. 'I believe in you,

Grace. I always have. You must go to Argentina to check this vineyard and its wine production for me.'

She was filled with concern for Elias and fear at the thought of failing him. 'I want to help, but—'

'Don't say *But I'm blind,*' Elias warned her. 'Don't ever say that, Grace, or everything you have achieved since losing your sight will be lost.'

'And you've been there for me from the start.'

'Yes, I have,' he said pointedly.

When he had first heard about her illness Elias had sought her out with an unconditional offer of help, saying it was his way of repaying Grace for all her small kindnesses over the years.

'You know how short we are on Argentinian wine,' he said. 'Would you have me turn customers away?'

'No, of course not. But do I really need to go to Argentina? Can't we find someone else to go?'

'No,' Elias said flatly. 'Apart from the little matter of trust, I think you need to go to Argentina to prove you can do it, Grace. It's the next step for you. And if you won't do it for yourself, then do it for me. I'm trying to make a businesswoman out of you, as well as a connoisseur of wine, and you must always satisfy yourself that things are what they seem to be before you place an order. It won't be so bad,' he encouraged. 'You'll only be there a month or so—'

'A *month!*' Grace exclaimed, horrorstruck. Just when she'd been about ready to say maybe, Elias had moved the goalposts.

'And you must leave right away, to catch the harvest at its best,' he continued. 'I'll need a full report from you, Grace.'

One of the things she loved about Elias was that he never made any allowances for her being blind. But this was too much. This wasn't the 'next step'—it was a huge leap across an unknowable chasm.

'But you know I can't travel—'

'I know nothing of the sort,' Elias argued. 'You can get about London, can't you?'

'Only because I have Buddy to help me—'

'Exactly,' Elias interrupted. 'Grace, I can't trust anyone else to do this. Are you saying I wasted my money training you?'

'Of course not. I can't imagine what I'd be doing now if you hadn't helped me. You know how grateful I am.'

'I don't want your gratitude. I want you out there doing the job you've been trained to do.'

'But I haven't left the country since—'

'Since your sight was reduced to looking at the world as if through the wrong end of a telescope? Yes, I know that. But I thought you liked a challenge, Grace?'

'I do,' Grace insisted, remembering the staff at the rehabilitation centre telling her she must keep pushing the boundaries—but not as far as Argentina, surely?

'I can't travel,' Elias said flatly, 'and taking on a new supplier is a huge risk for the business. We have to be sure these wines are as good as they promise to be.'

'Surely sending me in your place is an even bigger risk?'

'Grace, my father taught me, his father taught him, and now I've trained *you,* with many patient tasting sessions—'

'Patient?' Grace interrupted, starting to smile.

'I love to hear you happy, Grace. Don't let life frighten you. Please promise me that.'

'But do I know enough?' she said, still fretting.

'I know sommeliers who have been judging wine for forty years and don't have your natural ability,' Elias insisted. 'There's only one amateur I can think of who comes close to matching your palate and he just left the building.'

Grace felt the same tremble of awareness she had felt at that dinner, when Buddy had started barking, but she didn't believe in coincidence, and there had to be more than one family in Argentina that owned vineyards. And hadn't Lucia said the Acosta vineyards had been languishing for years?

'You don't have to worry about Buddy,' Elias was saying. 'He won't be a problem as you'll both be travelling in style on the Acosta family jet.'

'The Acosta family?' Grace's throat closed up as her worst fears were confirmed. 'Who exactly is it I'm meeting in Argentina?' she managed hoarsely.

Elias laughed, as if to confirm his thoughts that she was overreacting. 'Don't worry, you don't have to face the whole tribe at once—just the kingpin, Nacho.'

'Nacho?' A sound that was half a laugh and half a hysterical sob squeezed out of her throat. 'You *have* warned Señor Acosta that I will be travelling to Argentina in your place?'

Elias took too long to answer.

'You haven't?' she said.

'I won't lose out to a competitor,' Elias said stubbornly. 'And I can't see why you're making such a fuss. You know the Acosta family, don't you?'

'You know I do. Lucia is my best friend. You must remember we worked together at the club. And, yes, I've met her brothers, too,' she said, making sure to keep all expression out of her voice.

'Well, there you are!' Elias exclaimed. 'You'll be flying to the far west of their property, where I'm told it's very beautiful. You'll see the snow-capped Andes, and all those glorious rivers that feed the vines. It's perfect wine-growing country—' Elias stopped. 'Oh, Grace, I'm so sorry...'

'Please don't be,' she said. 'What I can't see I can't tell you about, but I'll make up for it in other ways, I promise. I'm sure the air will be different—and I can still smell. I can still feel the sun on my face. And the rain,' she added wryly as the latest in a series of angry winter storms rattled the windows. 'There will be so many new experiences—' She stopped, remembering the one experience ahead that really frightened her: meeting the most formidable of the Acosta brothers again. 'Was Nacho Acosta here today, by any chance?'

'Yes. Nacho's taken charge of the family vineyards,' Elias confirmed breezily. 'I've got every confidence in you,' he stressed. 'I know I couldn't have a better representative. This trip is going to be a piece of cake for you, Grace.'

It was to be hoped the cake didn't choke her.

CHAPTER TWO

GRACE'S decision to go to Argentina had been made by the time Elias left the room. She wouldn't let her elderly mentor down. She'd always been thankful Elias didn't treat her any differently because she was blind, and now she had to rise to the challenge. It was just a little harder because Nacho was involved…

Okay, it was a whole lot harder. Nacho wasn't exactly noted for his tolerance, and this would be her first big job. Was she trying to run before she could walk? Would Nacho even listen to her views on his wine and the way he ran the family vineyard? Apart from the extensive training Elias had given her she had no real experience in this area, and certainly no money or lofty lineage like the Acosta family.

She must stop with the negatives and concentrate on the positives, Grace concluded. But her thoughts were all over the place at the thought of meeting Nacho again. Their first meeting had been a disaster, and her body had reeled at the sight of him, but this next meeting would be very different. It was business, and she didn't have the option to be a shrinking violet. Now she was blind she had to get out there and make her presence felt.

She thought back to the wedding again, and how

painfully shy she had been. She had felt out of place amongst so many glamorous, confident people, and had been horrified when Nacho had come to her rescue. She hadn't been able to think of anything interesting to say to him, and had stood transfixed like a rabbit trapped in a car's headlights when he had brushed a gentle kiss against her lips. First chance she'd got, she'd bolted. 'Like Cinderella,' as Lucia had later chided her, adding the un-settling news that her brother had been less than pleased.

Grace couldn't begin to imagine what Nacho would think of her now she was blind and also in a position to put a curb on his business objectives.

This wasn't the first time since her sight had failed that she had felt like beating her head against the wall and screaming, *Why me?* Unfortunately, she always came up with the same answer: why *not* me?

Later that night Grace packed a case with an as-sortment of clothes taken from her carefully organised wardrobe. Lucia, who had always been strong on the organisational front, had come up with a foolproof plan that enabled Grace to find colour-co-ordinated outfits. By tagging the various suit bags and drawers with Braille labels, Lucia had made finding her clothes and acces-sories easy.

If only handling inner turmoil could be managed as easily, Grace fretted.

She was excited and yet terrified at the prospect of seeing Nacho again. But she couldn't actually *see* him, so it couldn't be that bad.

Even she didn't believe that.

Not wanting to spoil Grace's chances of making the trip, Elias had e-mailed Nacho immediately to say that at the last minute another expert would be taking his place.

'Well, it's true,' Elias had protested when Grace had pulled him up on it.

Grace might not approve of Elias's methods, but he had her loyalty—and if she stopped to think how Nacho was going to react when he saw who it was taking Elias's place she would never get on that plane.

A blind sommelier? Wouldn't *that* be a thrill for Nacho? He was expecting Elias Silver, master vintner and emperor of a European wine distribution network, and he would get Grace and her guide dog instead.

The journey to Argentina was so much easier than Grace had imagined. A chauffeur-driven car picked her up at home, and her transit through the airport was seamless. Maybe that was something all private plane passengers experienced but, blind or not, she thought it was quite something to be escorted and fussed over.

The moment she stepped out of the plane she noticed how warm it was, and how good it felt to have the sun on her face instead of the prickly chill of a damp English winter. The smell of jet fuel still caught in her throat, but there was spice in the air too, and the foreign language sounded musical and intriguing.

There were interpreters on hand to lead Grace to yet another chauffeur-driven car, and the driver was chatty, spoke perfect English, and took a very obvious pride in his country—which led to an illuminating travelogue for Grace. Apparently there were billboards of the Acosta brothers all the way down the main road, and as they travelled across the flat expanses of the pampas he told her about the jagged mountains there, with eagles soaring on the updrafts around their snowy peaks.

The driver showed no surprise that Grace was blind.

Nacho's PA had made all the arrangements with Elias, he explained, when Grace made a casual comment. It was just the great man himself who didn't realise he had a beautiful woman coming to taste his wine, as Nacho had been away on a business trip, the driver joked.

Ha-ha, Grace thought weakly, but the driver went on to tell her about the broad river that flowed like a sinuous silver snake through emerald-green farmland until it passed the *hacienda*, where it roared down to a treacherous weir. Even if she could have seen everything the driver was describing to her, Grace began to think that she might have rested back after the long journey anyway, and allowed him to colour in the scenes outside the window for her.

It was a long drive to the vineyard, and she fell asleep after a while. When she woke she felt rested in mind and body, knowing the first hurdle—travel—was behind her. This was the first time she'd been abroad since losing her sight and she'd travelled halfway across the world! That should give her *some* confidence.

Remembering Elias's enthusiastic description of the vineyards, Grace realized she was looking forward to discovering them for herself. She might not be able to see all those wonderful sights, but she would hear the river the driver had told her about, and she would smell those lush emerald-green farmlands. She smiled, convinced that in spite of all the Nacho-sized problems ahead of her she was going to like it here.

His schedule had been ridiculous recently—one business trip on top of another—but when he visited this particular stretch of the river he began to relax.

It was like visiting a grave and speaking to his long-dead parents, Nacho reflected darkly.

When he had first returned to the vineyards every inch of the estate had taunted him with one painfully familiar scene after another, but he had continued to ride the paths until he had conquered the demons and made some sort of peace—enough, at least, to revive the vineyards. Perhaps he gained a sense of perspective in the shadow of the Andes, and all the small irritations in his life could be swept away in the broad silver river as it flowed to the sea.

Murmuring reassurances to his newly broken horse, he slapped the proud, arched neck with approval. When his stallion stilled to listen to his voice he wondered, not for the first time, if he didn't prefer animals to people. As the stallion struck the ground aggressively he was reminded they were both experiencing great change. The horse had lost his freedom, while Nacho had gained his after years of caring for his siblings. But the shallow life of a playboy had not been for him, and his freedom had soon proved disappointing. So Nacho had returned to Argentina full of renewed determination to turn the failing vineyards into a valuable asset for his family.

'We both need something to distract us,' he murmured as the stallion's muscles balled beneath him.

Keen to inspect the vines, he urged the horse forward. Under his rule order had been restored and another considerable asset added to the Acosta family fortune.

The sun on his back after the chill of London was an almost sensual pleasure, and he couldn't have been in a better mood. Until he saw the dog. Unleashed and unattended, a big yellow mutt was relieving himself on his vines. And then a flash of movement drew his attention to the riverbank. Filled with fury at this unauthorised intrusion, he kicked the horse into a gallop, closing the distance at brutal speed.

'This is private land!' he roared, drawing the stallion to a skidding halt.

Grace hugged herself in terror. That voice, the raging hooves—this was everything she had been dreading and more.

And everything she had hoped for, Grace's inner voice insisted.

Had *dreaded*, Grace argued firmly. She had planned to have a businesslike first meeting with Nacho, in the calm surroundings of his office—not the furious drum of steel-shod hooves crashing to a halt only inches away. His horse's hot breath was on her face, and she could feel Nacho glaring down at her. Being this close to him slammed into her senses and memories flooded back, colouring in the void behind her eyes. Nacho was bigger, stronger, darker—more intimidating than any man she had ever known before.

So had she wilfully courted danger? Hadn't Nacho's housekeeper warned her that the master might be back home soon? Hadn't she mentioned that he always liked to ride along the riverbank when he came home?

Nacho wheeled his snorting stallion to a halt within a few inches of the girl's back. She didn't flinch, as he had expected. She didn't move at all. She kept her back to him and ignored him. Her dog showed more sense, sinking to its belly and baring its teeth.

'This is a private land,' he repeated harshly, 'And you are trespassing.'

'I heard you, Nacho.'

Dios! Dear God! No!

As the girl turned around, shocked curses without number or form flooded his head. When he saw who it was…when he saw her unfocused eyes…*he knew her.*

Of course he knew her. But not like this.

'Grace?' he demanded.

'Of course it's Grace,' she said—with false bravado, he suspected, noticing how she quivered with apprehension like a doe at bay. 'Didn't Elias e-mail ahead to warn you I was coming?'

'My PA said something about his replacement.' His brain was racing to find the right words to say. There were none, he concluded. He was angry at this obvious deception by Elias, but he was shattered at seeing Grace like this.

'And you can't believe I'm that replacement?' she said. 'Is that it?'

'How can you be,' he demanded, 'when Elias is the best in his field?'

She fell silent and he took a better look at her. It felt strange to be staring at someone who couldn't see—as if he were taking advantage of her, almost. But apart from the vague, unfocused eyes Grace hadn't changed that much at all.

He didn't need this sort of distraction in his life. He had marked Grace out as interesting at Lucia's wedding, only to find her disappointingly immature and naïve.

'I'm sorry to disappoint you,' she said, crashing into his thoughts. 'I felt sure that Elias would have mentioned that I work for him when you came to see him in London.'

'The subject never came up,' he said brusquely. 'Why would it?'

'Well, please don't be angry with Elias. He trained me well, and he has every reason to trust my judgement.'

'And you expect *me* to?' Nacho cut in with scorn.

His horse had started stamping its hooves on the ground, as if the big beast had had enough of her too. She could smell it and feel its hot breath. She could hear the creak of leather and the chink of its bridle as it danced impatiently within inches of her toes.

'I can't believe Elias would send a young girl in his place when I was expecting a master vintner,' Nacho said from somewhere way above her.

'And you're wondering what I can possibly know about fine wine?' she said, determined to keep her voice steady.

'I'm wondering what you're doing here at all. Did you learn about wine at the club?' he suggested scornfully.

The wine they had served there, by Elias's own admission, had been his cheapest brand, Grace remembered.

'There's definitely been some mistake,' Nacho insisted.

'There's no mistake,' Grace insisted, growing angry. 'I can assure you I've been very well trained.'

Nacho laughed. 'So has my horse.'

She looked as if she'd like to unseat him, her jaw fixed and her hands balled into fists. She was angry. So what? But what should have been a simple solution—send Grace home on the next flight—was immeasurably changed by the fact that she was blind. And she was his sister's best friend. How could he rage against a girl scrabbling around on the ground searching for her dog's harness?

'It's over there—to your left,' he said impatiently.

Dios! What had he said now? Grace couldn't see anything to her left *or* her right.

'Thank you, but Buddy will find it for me,' she snapped, still angry with him.

Sure enough, the big dog put the harness in her hand.

The last time Nacho had seen Grace had been at Lucia's wedding, where he'd felt a connection between them he couldn't explain. Wanting to pursue it, he'd found her as nervous as a fawn. Perhaps she had sensed something of the darkness about him? he'd thought at the time. She had certainly changed since then—because she'd had to, he realised. There was a resolve about Grace now that piqued his interest all over again.

'I realise that my coming here must be a shock for you, Nacho,' she said. She deftly fastened the harness while the big dog stood obediently still.

'Somewhat,' he conceded, with massive understatement. 'What happened to you, Grace?'

'A virus,' she said with a shrug.

However casually she might treat it, he felt angry for her. 'How long do you plan to stay?' Before she had a chance to answer he gave his own reading of the situation. 'I expect you'll take a few notes, have a look around, and then report back to Elias. Shouldn't take long—say, a day?'

'A *day*?' she exclaimed. 'I'll need to do more than take a few notes!'

In spite of his outrage at the trick Elias had played on him, his overriding feeling was of dismay when Grace turned her head and her lovely eyes homed in on the *approximate* direction of his voice.

'I've brought a Braille keyboard and a screen with

me,' she explained matter-of-factly. 'I expect to be here for around a month.'

'A month?' he exploded.

'Possibly a couple of days more,' she said, thinking about it. 'Please don't be concerned,' she said briskly. 'I am a trained sommelier, with a diploma in viticulture—'

'And how much experience?' he demanded sharply. What the hell was Elias playing at? He would just have to send someone else to evaluate his wine.

Sensing his growing anger, the stallion skittered nervously beneath him. Grace had started walking up the path ahead of him, with her dog at her heels.

'Aren't you going to put your sandals on?' he called after her

'I'm not a child, Nacho.' Without turning she dangled her sandals from one finger and waggled them at him in defiance.

She couldn't let Nacho see that she was as tense as a board, and that she couldn't stand his scrutiny a moment longer. She just had to get back to the guest cottage where she was staying and regroup. She hadn't anticipated feeling that same stab of excitement when was she near him, but nothing had changed. Nacho couldn't have made it plainer that she was not only the last person he wanted to see but an unwelcome intruder on his land— and a fraud. At the wedding she had allowed her head to fill with immature fairytale notions and had had her bluff well and truly called when he had sought her out. But she was here now, and she was staying until she got this job done.

They walked on in silence. She felt as if Nacho were tracking her like a hunter with his prey. She could feel his gaze boring into her back, flooding every part of her with awareness and arousal. It made her recall his touch on her arm at the wedding and the brush of his lips on her mouth. She remembered the terrifying way her body had responded—violently, longingly. Common sense had kicked in just in time, reminding her that she was inexperienced and Nacho Acosta was not, and that any more kisses would only lead to heartbreak in the end. As far as Grace was concerned, love and lovemaking were inextricably entwined, while Nacho, according to the popular press, was a notorious playboy who drank his fill at every trough around the world.

But he was right about one thing. *If only she could see.*

The path was stony. She stopped to put her sandals on.

'Please don't,' she said, hearing Nacho move as if he might dismount to help her. 'Buddy will stop me falling,' she insisted—which should have been true. But for the first time in ages she was stumbling around *like a blind woman*. She hadn't felt so unsure of herself since the shadows had closed in, Grace realised, beginning to panic. She even missed when she went to grasp Buddy's harness.

'Here—let me,' Nacho said brusquely.

It was too late to say no. He had already sprung to the ground.

'Thank you, but you'll only confuse Buddy,' she said tensely, feeling quivers of awareness all over her body as Nacho closed in.

'My apologies,' he said in a cold voice. 'I realise your dog can do many things, but can he catch you if you fall?'

'Buddy prevents me falling,' she pointed out. 'And we're fine from here. Buddy? The cottage.'

She was walking faster and faster now, practically running from one kind of darkness to another, with no landmarks in between. She was frightened of the strange territory, and she was frightened of Nacho. She heard him mount up again and now he was right behind her, his horse almost on top of her.

'We know our way,' she insisted, fighting off the terrifying sense of being hunted in the dark. She wished he'd speak, so she could tell exactly where he was. She wished she could see his face and know exactly what he was thinking. As long as there wasn't any pity on it. She couldn't have borne that. She'd had enough of people treating her as if her brain was faulty along with her sight. 'Really, we're fine from here,' she called out, hating the fact that her voice was shaking.

'Can't I show you some basic civility?' he said, giving her some indication that he was keeping his horse a safe distance away. 'While you're here in Argentina you're my guest.'

While she was there? That sounded ominous, as if she wouldn't be here very long—which was bad news for Elias. 'Look, I must apologise,' she said, drawing to a halt. 'I realise we haven't got off to the best of starts. I want you to know that I'm really looking forward to tasting your wines…' She stood and listened. It had gone very quiet again. 'Elias spoke so highly of them…'

She breathed a sigh of relief as she heard Nacho's horse move and its harness chink.

'I'm sorry if my being here instead of Elias has been a disappointment for you,' she said.

Not half as sorry as he was.

'And I realise you must be wondering—'

'Wondering *what*, Grace?' he interrupted. Shortening the reins, he brought the stallion under control. 'Elias has kept me completely in the dark. I feel let down. What am I supposed to think when Elias sends a young girl with little or no experience in his place? If you're asking me to be blunt, I can't imagine how you can possibly do the job.'

She flinched, and he felt wretched, but people's livelihoods were at stake. And now she was about to fall down a bank.

'Grace, watch out!' he yelled.

'I'm not going anywhere,' she said as the dog led her safely back onto the path.

'You nearly did.'

'Buddy wouldn't let me fall.'

He admired her confidence and hoped it wasn't misplaced. This was not the naïve young girl he remembered from Lucia's wedding. This was a woman with steel in her spine and she intrigued him—which complicated matters.

'How did you find your way to the river in the first place?' he said, trying to imagine himself blindfolded, with only a dog to lead him.

'Buddy heard the water—smelled it too, I expect. He started barking, and after the long journey I thought we both needed some fresh air.'

'I can't understand why my sister didn't mention your illness.'

'Because I asked her not to.'

'Why keep it a secret?' he said suspiciously.

'Because I'm handling it,' she said, marching on. 'Because I don't want to be treated any differently just because I can't see. I don't want to be defined by being blind. I don't want it to influence what people think about me.'

'I think you're being overly optimistic, Grace.'

'Well, maybe I am, but I don't want smothering,' she snapped. 'I'm quite capable of looking after myself.'

'Don't you think it would be more considerate if you warned people in advance, so that they can make the necessary provision for you?'

'What provision?' she flashed. 'That's exactly what I *don't* want. Why should I—?'

'Compromise?' he suggested as he battled to keep the stallion in check.

The horse was bored with inactivity, and it didn't like the turn this conversation was taking. Animals could sense tempers rising faster than humans, and Nacho was determined that passions of any kind would not be roused between him and Grace.

Passion could kill, as he knew only too well, and he never made the same mistake twice.

CHAPTER THREE

'SURELY compromise is all part of adapting to your new situation?' Nacho insisted as he continued to follow Grace along the riverbank. He caught a glimpse of her face as she strode along. Her jaw was firm and the set of her face was still angry. He could almost see her thinking, *What would you know about it?* And the answer to that, for once in his life, was absolutely nothing.

'Why should I compromise?' she said, confirming those thoughts. 'That sounds too much like defeat to me.'

'Grace! Watch that branch—'

'I'm okay,' she fired back, and the big dog adjusted direction seamlessly to lead Grace safely round the fallen branch.

But she still couldn't know she was so very close to the edge of a steep bank, or that from there it was just a short fall into the fast-flowing river. Nacho's head reeled with sudden dread as he thought back to another time and a tragedy he should have been there to prevent.

'I might not be able to see the river,' Grace said, as if she could read his thoughts as well. 'But I can hear it. And with Buddy to guide me and keep me safe—'

'There's absolutely no danger of you falling in?' he demanded sarcastically as the ugly memories continued to play out in his head. 'And if such a thing were to happen, your dog would, of course, leap in and save you.'

'Yes, he would,' she said, ignoring his sarcasm. 'Buddy has more ability than you can possibly imagine.'

His imagination was all too active, unfortunately, and while Grace was staying here she was *his* responsibility. 'Next time you feel like putting your life at risk, call me first.'

He ground his jaw when she laughed. It would be better if Grace left immediately.

'I'm sorry if I shock you with my independence,' she said. 'Would you have preferred me to remain cowering in the guest cottage until you arrived?'

'If you expect to do any sort of business with me you should think firstly about being more polite, and secondly about being more compliant.'

'More compliant? What do you think I *am*? And if you speak like that to everyone you meet, no wonder they're not polite to you. My job, as I understand it, is to independently judge your wine—so I would have thought that for your sake, and for the success of your business, my *compliance* would be the last thing you should want.'

She had an answer for everything. His practised gaze roved over Grace's slender frame. She had changed completely in all ways but one—physically she was every bit as attractive as he remembered.

'Elias has been very good to you,' he observed, curious about this new Grace.

'Yes,' she said, relaxing for the first time. 'He took me on when no one else would even give me a job. And he paid for my training.'

It was interesting to see her open up, though the training must have been recent, which was hardly what he hoped for in an expert. 'I'm surprised Elias was less than frank with me. He only had to pick up the phone to explain what he intended to do.'

'And would you have allowed me to come if he had done that?'

He had no answer to that.

'And please don't blame your PA,' Grace insisted. 'You must have been in the air when Elias e-mailed. Your housekeepers have made me very welcome, so it would seem she has done her job to perfection.'

His PA *had* called him, but he'd hardly been listening. One of the old-timers at the business meeting he'd been attending had been telling him that Nacho's visit to London had reminded them all of the old days—when his father had gone tomcatting around Europe, he presumed. Nacho had wanted to defend himself, to protest that that might have been his father's way but it wasn't his, but he wouldn't betray his father. The conversation had taken him back to being a boy, standing tall and proud in front of his parent, and being told that Nacho would be in charge of the family while his father was away.

It was only at school that he had learned the truth. His parents weren't the only ones who had been good at keeping secrets. Nacho had kept secrets most of his life.

'You *won't* blame your PA for this, will you?' Grace pressed him.

'No, of course not,' he said, frowning as his thoughts snapped back to the present and Grace.

She nodded her thanks as she continued to walk confidently behind the dog.

She might have been on a footpath in London rather than a remote trail in the shadow of the Andes.

How could she know the difference?

Whatever he thought of Grace arriving in Elias's place, it was impossible not to rage against her fate.

'The air's so good here,' she enthused, oblivious to his thoughts as she sucked in a deep, appreciative breath. 'It's like the finest wine: crisp and ripe, laced with the scent of young fruit and fresh blossom.'

His expression changed. Perfect. A romantic. Wasn't that all he needed in a business associate? Not that Grace would be around long enough to do business with him. As soon as he could politely get rid of her he would.

But as the wind kicked up, lifting her glossy blonde hair from her shoulders, he felt exactly the same punch in the gut attraction he'd felt at the wedding.

Turning towards the mountains, he searched for distraction. The Andes were always a glorious sight—a towering reminder of the majesty of the land entrusted to him. It was a trust that even the most bitter of memories couldn't alter. The rugged peaks sheltered his vines from the worst of the weather, while the glacier-melt flowing down the slopes of those peaks sweetened the glistening purple grapes.

And Grace could see none of it...

Meeting a beautiful young woman in the first flush of her beauty and wanting her, and then barely two years later seeing her like this, was a stinging reminder that nothing in life remained the same.

'Your housekeeper mentioned you had business in South Africa?' Grace said, obviously in an attempt to get the conversation going again.

'I was there on business,' he said curtly.

No wonder Nacho had a reputation for being the most difficult of the Acosta brothers. But Grace thought she could see a reason for it. As the oldest child, responsible for his siblings, Nacho hadn't had much time for himself. Even on the polo field he was the leader of the pack, with all the responsibility that involved.

She tried again. 'I hope my using your family jet didn't leave you slumming it on a scheduled flight?'

'I'm not that precious, Grace.'

As she laughed Grace turned her head in the direction of his voice. Another solid blow to the gut hit him when he saw that gaze, so lovely, yet so misty and unfocused, miss his face. He stamped on the feeling it gave him. Grace was his responsibility only while she was here. Once she was gone that was an end of it—and she wouldn't thank him for his pity.

'Are you still there?' she called out.

'Battling to keep up,' he mocked, riding with the reins hanging loose. He had kicked his feet out of the stirrups some way back.

'You're very quiet,' she said, marching on.

'You'll know when I've got something to say.' He stared at her back—the upright stance, the pitch of her head, chin lifted. He couldn't get over how confident she had become.

Because she'd had to.

'Just let me know if I'm going too fast for you,' she mocked.

She made it hard for him to remain angry for long. In fact she reminded him in some ways of his sister, Lucia. Lucia was always pushing the boundaries, always testing him, and he could see now why the two girls were such good friends.

'I can see you have picked up some very bad habits from Lucia. And as you're not my sister, and merely work for me—'

'*With* you,' she flashed.

'As you're not my sister,' he repeated patiently, 'your privileges do not extend to goading me while you're here.'

'So you *have* accepted that I am going to be here for a while?'

'I didn't say that.'

'You didn't have to.'

This time when she turned her head in his direction he saw the smile hovering round her mouth. His gaze remained on her lips for quite some time.

'Can I ask you something, Nacho?' she said, turning back again.

'Of course,' he said, feeling the loss now he had to content himself with a view of the back of her head.

'Will you give me a list of all the places that are out of bounds so I don't make any more mistakes? In Braille, of course,' she added, tongue in cheek.

A muscle worked in his jaw. He wasn't used to this sort of insubordination. Most people obeyed him gladly. 'I'll tell you what I'll do,' he said, realising that he was going to have to play Grace's game for the short time she was here. 'I'll get a translator for you. Or you could learn my rules by rote, if you prefer.'

'Are you smiling?' she said. 'I can't tell.'

No. He was learning fast and had kept his voice carefully neutral.

'If this visit is going to be a success,' she said, bearing out his theory, 'we'll both have to make adjustments—won't we, Nacho?'

'Will we?' he said.

The breeze was on Grace's side. Catching hold of the hem of her flimsy summer dress, it flicked it, giving him a grandstand view of her smooth, tanned legs. Arousal fired inside him, but he instantly damped it down.

'Do you remember when we first met in Cornwall?' she said, pulling his attention back to her hips as she strode along. 'You had just arrived for that polo match

on the beach. You rolled down the window of that monster Jeep, and—'

'And what, Grace?' he pressed, seeing her cheeks
had flushed bright red. A very masculine hunger filled
him at the thought that she had wanted him back then.

'I was just wondering if you remembered, that's all,'
she said casually, closing the topic with a flick of her
wrist.

He remembered.

When Grace fell silent it gave them both a chance to
think back. She broke the silence first. 'I could see you
properly then.'

Very cleverly, she gave him no clue as to whether
that had been good or bad. 'You'll be pleased to know I
haven't changed—'

'Hard luck,' she flashed.

How was it possible to ignore a woman like this? Or
ignore the way she made him feel? No woman had made
him laugh in what seemed like forever. He was glad
the so-called appeal of the Acosta brothers was lost on
Grace, and he would be happy if he never had to hear
again in his life that he looked like his father. His gaze
returned to Grace's slender hips, swaying to a rhythm
that was all her own. One thing was certain: if this banter between them was a ruse to keep his interest, she had
succeeded where many had failed.

'I was over-awed by you,' she admitted.

'Why?'

'Because you were so famous and seemed so aloof.
And even compared to the other polo players you were
huge—and so confident.'

'And at the wedding?'

'You frightened me half to death,' she admitted
bluntly.

He laughed for the second time in who knew how many years. 'So how do you feel about meeting me again, Grace?'

'Well, at least I can't see you this time,' she said.

Laughter was becoming a habit he would have to break if he was to retain his title as the hard man of the Acostas. 'And does that help?'

'It certainly does,' she said.

It was a good, brave answer, but he was suspicious and couldn't resist asking, 'So, are you here to pick up where we left off?'

'As I recall,' she countered, 'when we met at the wedding I was the one to leave.'

Correct. '*Touché*, Señorita Lundström.'

A blast of white-hot lust ripped through him when she angled her head as if to cast him a flirtatious glance—though of course she could do no such thing. He liked this verbal jousting. He liked the way Grace stood up for herself. And he liked Grace. A lot.

'Is something wrong?' she called back to him. 'You've gone very quiet…'

'I'm enjoying the day,' he said, thinking it wise to confine himself, as the British so often did, to talk of the weather.

'It *is* beautiful,' she agreed, stretching out her arms.

Her arms were beautiful—slender and lightly tanned. *Grace* was beautiful. He only wished she could see how beautiful the day was—but that was a ridiculous investment of concern on his part. As was his growing admiration for Grace. Far better he got this conversation back to business, where Grace was sure to fall short and disappoint him. Then he could send her packing, and that would be the end of a fantasy where he changed from a hard, unfeeling man into the sort of hero Grace might admire.

'Buddy's certainly enjoying the weather,' she said.

'Oh, good,' he said without enthusiasm.

He stared at the dog. The dog stared back at him. He loved animals, and they normally gravitated towards him—but not this one. The big dog's loyalty was firmly fixed in stone. Nacho's attention switched back to Grace. From the back you wouldn't know anything had changed about her. Life could be very cruel sometimes, but that didn't change the facts. What the hell had Elias been thinking? What use was a blind sommelier?

'So, tell me about your job, Grace,' he said, starting to seethe as he thought about how he'd been duped by the wily old wine importer. 'How does that work?'

'What do you mean, how does it work?' she said without breaking stride. 'I might be blind, but I can still taste and smell.'

'And what about the clarity of the wine?' he pressed with increasing impatience. 'What about the sediment—the colour, the viscosity?'

'The colour I have to take on trust, when people describe it to me, but like most people I can detect sediment on my tongue. And I wouldn't expect to be offered thin or cloudy wine by anyone who took their wine seriously.'

Was that a dig at *him*? 'You seem very confident.'

'That's for you to judge when we hold the tastings.'

'We haven't got that far yet,' he reminded her, wondering if he had ever encountered this much resistance from a woman.

His gaze swept over her again. Subduing Grace would give him the greatest pleasure. And was something he would most certainly resist. He knew all about the long-term consequences resulting from impulsive actions, and he had no intention of travelling down that road again.

'Why else would I be here if not to taste your wine?' she said. 'Elias can't wait to get my verdict—and not just on your wines but on the way you produce them too.'

He heard the dip in her voice. Was she holding him to ransom so she could stay and do her job? The thought of being judged by Grace was anathema to him, but her employer, Elias, was not only one of the most respected voices in the wine industry, he was the biggest distributor in Europe. Nacho needed him. Bottom line? He couldn't risk offending Elias. But Grace had neither the experience nor the wisdom for this work. How could she match a man like Elias, who had a lifetime devoted to the development of top-quality wine?

'I know what you're thinking,' she called back. 'And I understand the reasons why you want to send me home. I apologise again if I don't fit the mould of expert you were expecting, but you should know I take my work extremely seriously and I'm very good at it—which is why Elias trusts me to do this job. Why don't you wait until you've seen me in action before you act as judge and jury and send me home?'

Was he that obvious? And as for seeing Grace in action—

Kill those thoughts. Being much younger than he was, *and* his sister's best friend, meant Grace occupied a very privileged position—not that she would ever know that.

Her dog had slowed as they approached the white picket fence marking the boundary of the guest cottage, and as Grace reached out at fence height in answer to some unseen tension on the guide dog's harness she said, 'Thank you for escorting us home, but we can take it from here...'

She was dismissing him? His gaze hardened. What if he wasn't ready to go?

Those thoughts were turned on their head by the sight of Grace tracing each blunt tip of the fence with her fingertips as she made her way to the gate. Her independence and her vulnerability touched him somewhere deep.

Having reached the gate, she was feeling for the latch. A shiver coursed down his spine at the thought of the darkness surrounding her. His instinct was always to protect and defend, so he dismounted—only to be dismissed with a blithe, 'See you later, Nacho...'

'I'll see you in,' he argued firmly. Grace was on foreign soil, and the little he knew about blindness said familiarity was everything where confidence and safety were concerned.

Opening the gate, he walked ahead of her to the front door. They'd talked the whole way, he realised, and yet his head was still full of questions: *How long were you ill? Did your sight fade quickly or slowly? How long did it take you to regain your confidence? How long have you had the dog? How much can you see—if anything?*

'It's very chivalrous of you, Nacho,' she said, pressing back against the door as if to keep him out, 'but it's really not necessary. I can manage perfectly well on my own from here.'

'Please allow me to decide what is and isn't necessary,' he said, and reaching past her opened the front door. He didn't play second in command to anyone. He'd taken the lead all his life and that was how it would stay.

'Goodbye, Nacho.'

Before he knew what was happening Grace had felt the gap between him and the door and had slipped through it with the dog at her heels.

The door closed.

So she had no more need of him? Good. He should be pleased.

He wasn't pleased.

Springing back onto his horse, he wheeled it round and galloped off.

CHAPTER FOUR

HE WAS still overheated from his exchange with Grace when he got back to the *hacienda*. The call he made to Elias would be straightforward. All he had to do was explain that Grace would be on the next flight home, and that if Elias couldn't provide an acceptable replacement Nacho would have no alternative but to look elsewhere for an expert to evaluate his wine. His hope was that it might be possible to keep Elias on board as a distributor and find an expert in whom they could both place their trust.

He should have known life was never that simple…

A coward? He had never been called a coward before by anyone—let alone by an elderly wine merchant.

A misogynist? Okay. Maybe he'd been called that a few times.

Safe to say, the conversation with Elias didn't go well.

Was Nacho referring to his Grace? Elias asked. Did Nacho dare to condemn Grace before even giving her a chance to prove herself?

All this was said on a rising cadence of wrath.

Was Nacho bigoted? Was he prejudiced against visually challenged individuals? Or was he frightened to put his wines to the test by a true expert, perhaps? Should

Elias be seriously concerned? Did Elias even have time for this nonsense?

And Nacho's answer...?

He subscribed to none of the above. He was the least prejudiced individual he knew.

He handled Elias coolly, remembering that the last time he had given free rein to his feelings the day had ended in tragedy.

'Give Grace a chance,' Elias insisted. 'You won't be disappointed.'

What did he have to lose? He could be looking for another expert while Grace did as much as she could do, he reasoned.

Having allowed Elias sufficient time to vent his anger, he ended the call with a reassurance that for Elias's sake he would give Grace another few days.

'That's too kind of you, I'm sure,' Elias snapped, and he cut the line—but not before Nacho heard the want and need in the other man's voice. They both needed something from the other, so for now Grace was staying.

And so the games begin, he thought as he stowed the phone. But, however intriguing he found Grace, he would send her home before intrigue turned to something more. If he had learned anything from the past it was that women could appear strong and then disappoint in ways that led to disaster.

Dismounting his horse at the gate of the cottage where Grace was staying, Nacho lashed the reins to the fence. Striding up the path, he rapped firmly on the door. The dog answered with a bark. Steadying his breathing, Nacho heard Grace's murmured thanks to Buddy in a voice that was gentle and affectionate, and then he heard her footsteps crossing the room to open the door.

'Nacho,' she said, in a very different tone from the one she'd used for the dog as she swung the door wide.

'You knew it was me?'

Coming straight from his call to Elias, Nacho was strung tight as a drum.

Sensing this, Grace lifted her chin. 'I will always know when it's you. Your horse has a distinctive stride. And the way you knock on the door is quite unique. I'm surprised it's still standing. And I could feel your tension a mile away—'

'My *what*?' he said.

'Exactly,' she said. 'So, what can I do for you, Nacho?'

No other woman spoke to him like this—with the possible exception of his sister, Lucia. Was this aloof attitude some defence mechanism Grace had perfected since going blind? Did she push everyone away now?

'You should move into the main house,' he said brusquely.

He had already turned and was on his way, having anticipated Grace's immediate compliance—her gratitude, even.

'Is that your acceptance speech?' she said, calling him back. 'Have you been speaking to Elias, by any chance?'

'You've spoken to him too?' he said.

'I might have done,' she fudged. 'So, am I to stay, Nacho? Is this your invitation?'

'I suppose you could call it one,' he conceded brusquely.

'But why would you want me to move into the main house?'

'Because you'll get the assistance you need there, obviously.'

'I beg your pardon?' she said.

'You'll be more comfortable,' he explained impatiently, knowing he should try to be more diplomatic.

'I'm very comfortable where I am, thank you,' she said coolly. 'And I wouldn't dream of inconveniencing you.'

'Don't be so ridiculous, Grace. How would you be inconveniencing me?'

'By making you more angry than you are now? By having you walk on eggshells during my stay? By making you feel duty-bound to watch over me?' She finished the tirade with an angry gesture. 'How much more time must I waste convincing you that I don't need any special treatment, Nacho?'

'How much time would *you* waste?' he fired back incredulously.

'Haven't you got it yet?' she said. 'I'm completely independent.'

'Don't tell me what to think, Grace,' he warned. 'If you're going to work for me, I'll show you the same consideration I show all my staff and not one iota more. Unless, of course, you're looking for pity?'

'Well, thanks for the heads-up,' she flashed, 'but I'm not working for *you*. I'm working for Elias. And if I were looking for pity—which I'm not—you would be the last person I'd turn to.'

He took a step back as she slammed the door in his face. Raking his hair with angry fingers, he was forced to admit that she'd got one thing right—he was the last person she *should* turn to. But that didn't change anything. His mind was made up.

Balling his fist, he hammered on the door.

'What now?' Grace demanded, flinging it wide.

'Do you mind if I come in for a moment?'

'It's your guest cottage,' she reminded him with a shrug. She stood well clear as Nacho walked in, and was glad of Buddy's warm presence nestling protectively against her legs. Closing the door after him, she heard Nacho start to pace. The room seemed smaller suddenly, and the air swirled around him as if it were in turmoil too.

No one had ever affected her like this. No one had ever frightened her quite so much, or made her want things so much she couldn't think straight. She'd been a fool to imagine she could ever do business with Nacho as if they had never met—as if she had never felt his hands on her arms or his lips on her mouth.

'I can see you're coping really well, Grace.'

Not right now she wasn't.

'Please don't patronise me,' she flashed. 'And please don't feel you must make a speech. There are people far worse off than me who pick up their lives and get on with things. I don't need your sympathy, Nacho. I'm here to do a job. All I ask is that you treat me like anyone else and make no allowances. You don't even have to be around while I'm working. I'm quite happy to liaise with your people and with Elias back home. I can draw up a report and send it to you as soon as we're finished. You don't even have to know I'm here.'

'Grace, please sit down.'

'I prefer to stand, if you don't mind,' she said, keeping the back of the chair between them like a shield.

'As you wish. You're right. I have spoken to Elias and we have agreed that you may taste the wine.'

'Really?' For the sake of her old friend she somehow managed to hide her affront.

'And when you've finished the tasting,' Nacho went on, 'I'll arrange for your flight home.'

'There's more to this job than tasting wine.' She was in turmoil, and her promise to Elias hung by a thread.

Her body was pulled one way by Nacho's sheer magnetism, while her mind was being pulled another. She wanted to stay, to experience more of Nacho, and yet she wanted to tell him to go to hell. She forced her thoughts back to business. 'Elias needs a lot more information before he's in a position to place an order.'

'Enough,' Nacho said firmly. 'That is all.'

'Are you firing me?' Before he had chance to answer, she demanded, 'On what grounds?' Her resolve to remain calm and concentrate on business had completely vanished as her anger increased. 'You haven't even given me a chance to prove myself.'

'I don't have time to waste on a novice. And I won't take chances with family money. I need an expert *now*, Grace.'

'So let me get this straight. You're prepared to allow me to taste the wine, but any comment I make will be classified as one amateur chatting informally to another?'

'I'm sorry, Grace. I realise how disappointed you must be.'

'You have no idea,' she said bitterly.

'Please don't worry about your homeward journey,' Nacho went on, as if she hadn't spoken. 'You will be flown home in my jet, and I'll smooth your path at the other end—'

'I don't need you or anyone else to *smooth my path,*' she interrupted angrily. 'Believe it or not, Nacho, I've been doing very well on my own without your help. I'm quite capable of booking a scheduled flight and having a cab take me to the airport!'

'And your dog?'

Grace went still. Hadn't they warned her at the rehabilitation centre to always give herself time to think? Couldn't she see why now? 'I'm sure I can arrange something,' she insisted, her stomach churning as she hoped that was true.

'There's no need,' Nacho assured her calmly. 'It's all in hand. And you don't have to worry about Elias, either. I'll explain that you didn't feel ready for an assignment of this size.'

'And he'll laugh in your face,' she said, realising time was running out as she heard Nacho's hand on the door handle. Against all that was sensible she wanted— needed—him to stay.

'My decision on this is final, Grace.'

'You're making a big mistake.' Following the sound of his voice she put her hand on his arm—only to draw it back again as if she had been burned.

'It's a job that's too big for you, Grace,' Nacho argued. 'Elias expects too much of you. And the outcome is far too vital for me to take a chance—'

'On a blind woman?' she flashed.

Silence greeted this, even as shame scorched her cheeks. That had been a low blow, and one she had promised herself she would never resort to.

'You disappoint me, Grace,' Nacho said quietly. 'I was about to say for me to take a chance on a novice like you. Restoring the family vineyards is a multi-million-dollar venture and I won't risk failure.'

'Which is why you consulted Elias, presumably?' she said, playing her last card. The thought of leaving this job unfinished, of leaving with her tail between her legs—the thought of leaving Nacho and maybe never seeing him again—was devastating to her. 'Don't you trust Elias's judgement?'

'Up to the point where we met in London—and then Elias conveniently forgot to tell me that he wouldn't be coming to view the vineyards himself.'

'He hasn't been well recently.'

Silence told her that Nacho had had no idea about this.

'I only saw him recently,' he said in a puzzled tone.

'He hides it well,' she admitted.

Shifting position, Nacho exhaled heavily. 'I'm sorry to hear that.'

But not sorry enough to change his mind, Grace concluded, hearing the door open. Nacho was happy to accept the judgement of a master vintner like Elias, but he was not prepared to listen to a girl he associated with nightclubs, silly costumes and trays of drinks.

With nothing left to lose, she said, 'As my time here is short, shall we get the wine-tasting done tonight?' The only way to convince Nacho she had anything to offer was to prove herself to him.

The door squeaked, as if he were pulling it to again, which she took to be a good sign.

'How about a blind tasting?' she suggested without a trace of irony. 'Elias warned you have a very fine palate...for an amateur.'

'Are you insulting me? Or is that meant to be a compliment?'

Was that a touch of humour in Nacho's voice at last? Her body heated at the thought while her mind told her to remain focused on her job. 'I thought it might appeal to your competitive spirit,' she said innocently, dragging greedily on the scent of warm, clean Nacho.

'Go on,' he prompted.

She heard the door click shut. 'I'm inviting you to share a sensory evaluation of your wine with me.' Why did that sound so suggestive and risky? She pressed on. 'You'll have the advantage of sight, while I can only use my other senses.'

'How many advantages do you think I need, Grace?'

Nacho's voice was carefully neutral, but she suspected he had decided to accept her challenge. 'This will be your chance to discover if I'm as good as Elias says I am.'

'Okay,' he said. But just when she was silently rejoicing he added, 'Pack your case and if you fail you'll be ready to leave.'

'I won't fail,' she said, firming her jaw.

'I guess we'll find out tonight, Grace,' Nacho murmured, sounding utterly confident that the result would go in his favour.

She felt the cool night air on her face as he opened the door.

'I'll be back to collect you at six,' he said.

'And I'll be ready for you,' she promised as she moved towards the door.

With a gasp she stumbled over a chair leg, and would have fallen to the floor if Nacho hadn't caught her.

'Grace—'

She was in his arms, which felt so good, so safe, so right. But it wasn't supposed to be like this. Nacho wasn't supposed to be rescuing her because she couldn't see where she was going. The only time she wanted him to hold her like this was under very different circumstances. And that clearly wasn't going to happen...

She pulled herself upright.

'Sit down, Grace. Catch your breath,' he said, stepping back.

The cold tone in Nacho's voice told her everything she needed to know. He had been as far from being about to

kiss her as it was possible to get. Why would he want a
blind woman when he could have any woman?

'Goodbye, Grace.'

He closed the door carefully behind him—and then
hit the wall backhanded with his fist. He barely felt
the blow. All he felt was Grace—in every part of him.
However hard he tried to fight off the feeling, Grace
fought back with her indomitable spirit, her unique quali-
ties, and her sheer unadulterated sex appeal.

Saving Grace when she'd stumbled had only reminded
him how attractive she was—and how emotionally in-
convenient spending time with her this evening would be
for him. The thought of kissing Grace had lost none of
its appeal, and if he hadn't seen first hand how one rash
decision could spread disaster like ripples on a pond he
would have done more than kiss her. But he had enough
on his conscience already without yielding to his every
whim.

Her world seemed darker than ever now Nacho had gone.
She curled up in a chair with her thoughts in pieces.
Mostly they were centred on her arms, where he'd held
her, and on her mouth, where he *hadn't* kissed her.

Why would he? Why would anyone want to kiss a
blind woman? She could prove herself to as many people in as many ways as she wanted, but she could never
get past the fact that she was blind. That was how people
saw her—how they would always see her—how Nacho
would always see her. The joke of it was she had forgotten she was blind while she had been with him. She'd
smiled and laughed and parried his comments, even got
angry with him—all of which had felt perfectly normal
and exciting. He'd made her forget what she might be

missing out on and had filled her world with so much more besides.

But now he'd left it was as if that light had gone out and now there was nothing but darkness around her again. And fear was back, fierce and strong, and fear said no one would ever see past her blindness.

CHAPTER FIVE

IT WAS no use. Feeling sorry for herself would get her absolutely nowhere. She held the record for proof of that. She had to get on with things.

The room was becoming increasingly chilly, which meant the sun was close to setting—which in turn meant Nacho would soon be back to take her to the wine-tasting. Whatever had happened between them—now or at the wedding—her job came first, and she was going to look the part by the time he knocked on the door.

Getting ready for a night out wasn't so different these days from the way it used to be—other than the thought of spending a whole evening in close proximity to Nacho, which put her on edge. She would just have to get over it, Grace reasoned.

Having showered and rubbed her hair dry on a towel in the bathroom she had mapped out carefully when she had first arrived, she dressed in what—thanks to Lucia's system—she knew was a pair of white capris, flesh-coloured sandals and a pale blue, short-sleeved cotton top. She smoothed her hair and tied it back. Make-up was easy. She'd been lucky in that she'd had some warning her sight was going, so she'd had a chance to practise her technique.

It was so easy for her now that she could actually do

her make-up without even thinking about it, Grace reflected wryly as she slicked some gloss on her bottom
lip and pressed her lips together. Her cheeks felt hot
enough from the thought of seeing Nacho again not to
need any rouge, and she was lucky to have been born
with black eyelashes. But she still liked her eyeshadow.
Two sweeps of the small brush across the pot, blow on
brush, apply, repeat. In the early days Lucia had used
to stand ready with wet wipes to correct any errors, but
then one day Lucia had done nothing, and they had both
shrieked in triumph as they threw their arms around each
other and hugged.

A sharp bark from Buddy warned Grace that her visi-
tor had arrived. Carefully feeling her way downstairs,
she paused to draw in a steadying breath before opening the door. That bolt of excitement—the way her heart
reacted when Nacho was close by—had nothing to do
with being blind and everything to do with Nacho. Just
the thought of being close to him again made her world
tilt on its axis. She didn't want his pity for being blind,
but even more than that she didn't want him thinking
she was an impressionable female incapable of function-
ing normally and doing her job while he was around.

'Well, this is it, Buddy,' she said, firming her jaw.
'We're all set.'

She opened the door and the breath left her lungs in
a rush. So much for her good intentions, Grace thought,
taking a moment to get over the Nacho effect.

'Grace…'

No matter how cool Nacho's greeting, the masculin-
ity firing off him was hot, hot, hot. She knew he was
towering over her, staring down, and she knew he was
very close.

'Hi…' She spoke brightly, with a smile, trying to sound as if this were a regular day at the office.

But it didn't work, she realised when he didn't speak. Her cheeks fired red. This was like stepping out into the void without a safety net. She couldn't really tell if she'd managed to dress and put her make up on without making too many goofs. Her hair might be standing on end for all she knew. She smoothed it self-consciously.

'Ready to go, Grace?'

'Yes, of course.'

Her throat felt tight as she reached for her briefcase. That was a small victory. She heard Nacho swoop to get it for her, but she got there first. She rarely lost anything these days, because it was so crucial she knew where everything was, and she had left it ready. Hanging the strap crossways over her body, she called Buddy, found the handle of his harness and reached for the door.

Was the air actually fizzing with electricity as she walked past Nacho or was that all in her head?

He closed the door behind them, and somehow managed to be at the gate in front of them.

'The Jeep's ahead of you, Grace. Would you like me to put Buddy in the back?'

'That's all right. I'll do it.'

She was going to start as she meant to go on. This was business and she was going to do it right. She felt her way round to the back of the vehicle. It was already open, and she did a good job of loading Buddy. It was only when she came round to the passenger door that she hit a snag. She mapped the door time after time, with increasingly sweaty palms, but she still couldn't find the handle. She felt so stupid—so hot and bothered—so frustrated.

'I presume I'm allowed to do *this* much for you?'

She took a step back as the door opened. Did she appear *so* prickly and defensive? Grace wondered as Nacho helped her in.

The answer to that was yes. She wasn't cut out for the role of victim. But there was no reason to overreact to every little comment he made, either.

Feeling for the seat, she settled in and Nacho swung in beside her. When he closed the door she had the sense of being contained in a very small space with him. He was a huge physical presence, but then she had always known that. It was Nacho's physicality and energy rather than the sheer size of him getting to her now, and she was heating up all over just at the thought of his big body closing in on her own small frame. She could smell that he was still damp from the shower and had used some sort of menthol soap…or perhaps that was toothpaste? Anyway, he smelled really good.

Were her nipples erect? she wondered suddenly. Could she risk checking? She decided not, and crossed her arms over her chest instead as he started the engine and they moved off. She could imagine his powerful hands on the wheel, controlling their direction with the lightest of touches. The leather seats were big and comfortable. She explored hers discreetly, and then relaxed. The seats were huge. There was no chance they could rub up against each other accidentally.

'It's just a short drive to our newly refurbished wine facility,' Nacho explained. 'We could have walked there, but I thought you might be tired after the upheaval of the day.'

Now she couldn't tell if he was smiling, frowning, or even laughing at her. He'd cottoned on very quickly to the fact that she could read a lot from a voice and was becoming increasingly clever at masking his opinion.

'That's very thoughtful of you,' she replied, settling for not making anything of his comment. 'I'm looking forward to tasting the wines.'

'Viticulture in this area goes back centuries,' he said, going on to explain something of its history.

She breathed a sigh of relief, realising that Nacho was actually treating her like an intelligent human being. 'So you're the guardian of history around here?'

'That's a nice way to put it,' Nacho agreed, and this time there really was some warmth in his voice.

Her first compliment, Grace registered—not that she was looking for any. Especially as they made her cheeks burn red.

'I'm only sorry you won't be able to see the old buildings we've been restoring,' Nacho commented.

She was taken aback for a moment, but then she realised she appreciated his frankness. 'Don't worry,' she said. 'I process loads of mental images through my other senses. And don't forget I have a whole library of images to draw on from the days when I *could* see. I'm lucky in that respect.'

'Yes, you are,' he agreed.

For the first time she began to relax. Nacho's candour suited her. To be treated normally was exactly what she wanted.

'So, what are your impressions of Argentina so far, Grace?'

'Well, it's certainly lovely weather after a freezing cold British winter, and the people are very kind. And there are all sorts of wonderful new scents and sounds here.'

'Horses?' he suggested dryly.

'Different,' she said. 'And there's a sort of samba rhythm in the air.'

Nacho laughed. 'Still the romantic, Grace?'

Was she?

'Still mining for choice pieces of information to add to our forward promotion for your wines—if Elias places an order,' she said coolly.

They fell silent after that sally, each rebalancing their opinion of the other, she thought.

Cocooned in darkness, she was given a chance to think back to the first time she'd seen Nacho. She'd found him frighteningly attractive, and in particular had seen something incredible about his eyes. He had such a keen stare it had seemed to suck information from her brain, while Nacho's own thoughts remained guarded. She remembered he rode with a bandana to keep his unruly hair from his eyes. When she had first seen him dressed for polo, with that bandana instead of a helmet, she had thought he looked exactly like the king of the brigands as he led his team out. He was clearly the boss and everyone accepted his leadership.

Maybe it was that edge of danger about Nacho, that sense of him having seen things and done things that might shock her if she knew about them, that perversely made him all the more attractive. An inconvenience she would have to get over if she wanted to appear business-like tonight.

'Grace?'

'Sorry.' She rejigged her thoughts. 'I was just thinking—I mean, I was just trying to imagine your wine facility.'

'I'll describe it to you.'

'That would be great,' she said, surprised to find him so amenable. 'Is the river close by?'

'Why do you ask?'

His voice had changed completely. She could have

kicked herself. Of course she knew about the tragedy—everyone did—but there was something in Nacho's voice she hadn't heard before. Something that suggested that although his parents might have drowned in a flood there years ago the tragedy still affected him. What really surprised her was that Nacho had always appeared to be the ultimate in grounded men, but there was a strand of defensive anger in his voice, along with what could only be described as guilt and raw grief.

'So, I gather you like it here?' he said, changing the subject.

She guessed that was a welcome relief for him, and needed no encouragement to enthuse about her experience so far.

'Like it here? I *love* it,' she said impulsively. 'What was it like growing up on the pampas, Nacho?'

She had said something wrong again, Grace realised when the silence thickened.

'It was all sorts of hectic chaos,' he said at last.

'Go on,' she prompted, eager to keep the faltering conversation going.

'There was no privacy,' he said, revealing the other side to Lucia's coin.

It probably hadn't ever occurred to Lucia that her brothers had been fighting to express their individuality too.

'Not nearly as much freedom as you might expect,' Nacho went on. 'And nowhere to go. When you're young all you want is the city and the nightlife, and what you get here is miles of wilderness, mountains and the stars.'

'And because you were the oldest you always had to look after your brothers and sister?' Grace guessed. Grasping the nettle, she dived back into the past, where she suspected Nacho's ghosts lay. 'Lucia said that after your parents were killed you worked very hard at looking after them.'

'I did my best,' he said, clearly not willing to be drawn on this point.

'That must have been hard for you,' she probed.

'Not really,' he said, shifting restlessly in his seat. 'Lucia had the worst of it,' he said after a few moments. 'Growing up must have been hell for her, with four brothers looking over her shoulders.'

'God help her if she got a boyfriend, I suppose?' Grace suggested with a grin.

This time she could imagine Nacho's ironic expression as he murmured, 'So she told you?'

As the tension eased a little she decided she would have to be patient. They'd get around to talking about Nacho eventually—she'd make sure of it. 'What about your brothers?'

'Ruiz was the perfect student,' Nacho explained with a shrug in his voice. 'He was also the perfect son and the perfect brother. In fact Ruiz never put a foot wrong. He always knew how to get on with everyone and how to get his own way. Diego was the dark side of that coin— dangerous, some said, though I always thought that was overstated. Diego was just deep.'

'And what about the youngest? Kruz?' she pressed.

She heard Nacho scratch his cheek, the stubble resistant against his fingernail. 'Kruz was a handful...' He sighed. 'Kruz was always in trouble.'

'And you?' she slipped in, sensing that talking about Kruz was opening up a whole can of worms. Nacho would probably prefer talking about himself—as difficult as she knew he found that.

'Me?' he said. 'I spent most of my time getting Kruz out of trouble.'

'That's not what I meant and you know it,' she chided, realising he'd eluded her again.

'I know what you meant,' Nacho assured her. 'And all I'm prepared to say on that subject is that what you see is what you get with me, Grace.'

Right up to that moment she'd had no reason to disbelieve a word Nacho said, but now she did.

'The gates,' Nacho explained as the Jeep dropped a gear and began to slow. He brought it to a halt.

'They must be big gates,' Grace observed, noting the length of time it took for them to open.

Nacho confirmed this, and then the Jeep growled and they drove on.

'We're approaching the old buildings down a long, tree-lined drive,' he explained.

'It's brilliantly lit,' she said. 'One of the things I can still detect is a big change in light.' She felt she had to explain this as she sensed his surprise that she should know anything about the light levels. 'I'm really lucky in that I can still detect light. It has helped me to work out which way round I'm facing on many occasions. When you can't see anything much, you're happy to take what you can get.' She laughed, but Nacho was silent.

They drove in silence. She could imagine Nacho steering with just his thumb on the wheel at this low speed, perhaps sparing her a glance from time to time. She sensed he was totally relaxed and yet thoroughly observant—as he was on horseback, and as he had been at the wedding where they had kissed. Even when he was still she thought he gave off about the same level of threat as a sleeping tiger.

'The building is old—mellow stone,' he explained, breaking the silence as he brought the Jeep to a halt again. 'It's beautifully preserved. Right now the moonlight is making the stone glow a silvery-blue.'

'And the sun will turn it rose-pink in late afternoon,' she guessed. 'There's more light now,' she said with interest, sitting up. 'A different light.'

'Wrought-iron lanterns hanging either side of the main doors,' Nacho explained. 'They give off quite a strong glow. It makes the mullioned windows on either side of the door glitter. How am I doing, Grace?' he said with a hint of amusement as he applied the brake.

'Not bad,' she said with a small smile. 'And how about the front door? No, don't tell me. It's huge and arched... stout oak with iron studs?'

'Argentine sandalwood,' he explained. 'But otherwise that's not a bad description, Grace. Welcome to Viña Acosta.'

Where my trial by wine begins, she thought, releasing her safety belt.

She climbed down carefully when Nacho opened the door, guessing his hand was there to help her if she needed it. She avoided it in the interests of independence, but she did feel it brush her back, where it lit a series of little fires she couldn't ignore.

Nacho let Buddy out of the back of the Jeep and when the guide dog came to her side she attached the leash to Buddy's harness. 'We're all set,' she confirmed.

Nacho led her into a pleasantly warm entrance hall with a stone floor. It wasn't large. She could tell that by the way their voices bounced off the walls and were very quickly muffled. The smell was distinctive and familiar. It reminded her of the tasting room at the warehouse, but here she guessed the woodwork would be impregnated with centuries worth of fruit and must and skins and juice.

'This is the tasting room,' Nacho explained as he opened another door. 'There aren't any steps.'

Grace had already guessed as much from the way Buddy was leading her, but she thanked Nacho for the warning.

'If you'd like to sit down, Grace?'

Recognising this request, Buddy led her across an uneven stone floor to a wooden bench. He stopped when Grace felt it nudge her legs. She reached forward to feel for the table she knew must be there and, gauging the space in between bench and table, she slid into the seat. While she was unhitching Buddy's harness she heard a rug hit the floor.

'He might as well be comfortable while we do this,' Nacho explained.

She smiled, remembering Lucia telling her that where animals were concerned nothing was too much trouble for her brothers. But if you were human…? Basically, forget it.

Now she could hear glasses chinking, and bottles being moved around. 'Are we alone?'

'Absolutely,' Nacho confirmed as he put bottles on the table. 'I had some of these wines opened earlier.'

'Good idea,' she said, and knew that just when she should be at her most professional she was feeling disorientated again. This was a familiar feeling in new surroundings, and one she would have to conquer, but there wasn't time tonight. At least she was sitting down. It wouldn't be the first time she had tripped over something. Even with Buddy's help, she sometimes forgot her restrictions and went flying.

But that wasn't going to happen tonight, Grace reassured herself firmly.

'Buddy?'

Hearing the big dog shift position, she was pleased to note he wasn't too far away. Buddy knew he was still on duty, but he hadn't heard the imperative note in her voice that called him to action. She mapped the table in front of her, feeling for glasses and bottles and other hazards. She always put down mental markers so she could understand her surroundings better. She listened intently as Nacho poured. Even the sound wine made as it glugged from the bottle told a story.

As the sound of her rapid breathing compared to Nacho's steady inhalations told another, Grace realised, consciously steadying herself.

'Right. Are we ready?' he said. 'I've labelled the bottles and glasses on the bottom, so that I can't see them when you swap them round.'

'An even playing field,' she agreed.

She had to concentrate fiercely and not think about that husky voice with its intriguing accent, or those dark eyes watching her every move.

As she tasted the first sample she could only wish Nacho's thoughts were as easy to read as the wine. Elias had described him as a gifted amateur, and when it came to wine no doubt that was true, but where women were concerned Nacho was a master of his craft. It was a thought that made her tremble with awareness.

'Well?' he said. 'What do you think so far, Grace?'

What did she think? Where wine was concerned she was utterly confident. Where Nacho was concerned she was out of her depth.

'Grace?'

She tensed when he came to sit beside her on the bench. She hadn't expected that.

'Spit or swallow?' he said.

She almost laughed. Nacho's blunt question while

his hard thigh brushing hers was just the wake-up call she needed.

'At this initial informal tasting I'm going to drink a mouthful of each wine.' She explained why. 'I like to hold it in my mouth and then feel the wine run through me. My stomach usually has something useful to say. I'll need water and coffee beans—to clean my palate and clear my nose. Every sommelier has their own way of doing things and this is mine. Don't worry, I've brought them with me.' She reached into her bag.

'Whatever it takes,' Nacho agreed.

'Not bad,' she commented after tasting the first couple of wines. 'But not great. And don't even ask me to *touch* this one,' she added when Nacho pressed a third glass in her hand. The smell was enough to put her off. 'Please don't waste my time with cheap tricks or rejects. I thought time was important to both of us.'

She felt his surprise, though he made no comment. He was cool. She'd give him that.

She *wasn't* cool, and breath shot out of her lungs when their fingers touched over the next glass.

'Very good,' she said, recovering fast. Burying her nose, she inhaled deeply. 'This is really very good.' She lifted her chin and wished she could see Nacho to show him her enthusiasm.

'It's a deep cardinal-red with bluish purple tones,' he explained.

'Young,' she added, taking another sniff. 'Full of the scent of ripe black fruit...'

'And?' Nacho prompted.

'And very well balanced,' she said, sensing his face was very close. Swallowing deep, she tried to concentrate. 'This is one of the best young wines I've tasted this year.'

'I have another, older wine I think you're going to like...'

She relaxed as he pulled away, and yet ached with disappointment that he had.

More wine was poured. She heard Nacho take a sip and imagined him savouring the ruby liquid in his mouth. 'I hope you're not cheating.'

'I don't need to cheat, Grace. Here—taste this...'

Somewhere in the room a clock was ticking as the tension mounted between them.

'What do you think?' Nacho prompted, 'Do you like it?'

'Yes...' She straightened up. 'This is an exceptional wine. It's older, richer and more complex than any wine I've tasted in England. I can detect more than one variety of grape.' She named them.

'You have an extremely discerning palate, Grace.'

'Isn't that what you're paying me for?' she said with amusement.

He liked the fact that Grace stood up to him, but as she went on to describe traces of chocolate and cinnamon, with hints of blackcurrant and cherry, he liked her a lot more. Not because of her expertise in wine, but because of the way his thoughts were turning to ruby-red wine moistening beautifully drawn lips, and drinking from those lips before sinking his tongue deep into Grace's mouth to capture the last drop, before moving on to lap more wine from the soft swell of her belly.

With his mind happily employed, he spoke his thoughts out loud. 'Is there anything I can do to speed things up?'

'If you mean can I guarantee an order now?' she said, breaking the spell, 'I'm afraid the answer's no. I need to know a lot more about your production methods before we can reach that stage.'

He was disappointed in Grace's businesslike manner. He was more disappointed in that than in the fact that placing an order for his wine wasn't immediately forthcoming. The Acosta name generally provoked a certain type of response—and delay or refusal was unheard of. But not with Grace, it seemed.

His brooding gaze lingered on her face. She had stood out for him at Lucia's wedding amongst all the flashy birds of paradise and she was lovelier than ever now. He found her bewitching, and he knew there was steel lurking beneath that calm exterior, making the playing field between them more even. So where he might have stood off at one time, bound by respect and restraint, those barriers no longer stood between them.

'I can reassure you that so far everything looks very promising,' she said.

'I couldn't agree more,' he said.

Grace had missed the irony. Or had she? What was hiding behind that composed front? Familiar with secrets, he knew the signs and suspected Grace's brave front hid a world of self-doubt. It occurred to him then that she must have cried at some point about her loss of sight. She must have railed against her fate. Who had held her when she had broken down in tears? Had anyone? She reminded him of a wounded bird that was determined to survive—which made his recent thoughts seem like those of a cold-hearted predator wheeling overhead.

'The flavours of this wine are complex, and the aroma is particularly distinct,' she said, burying her nose and inhaling deeply.

'On that we're agreed,' he said, far more interested in watching Grace now than in tasting the wine.

'Then why are you frowning?' she said.

'Am I?'

'Don't deny it. I can hear it in your voice, Nacho.'

'I'll have to frown less,' he said.

When she laughed her soft blonde hair, which had only been loosely held, escaped the band she had tied it up in and came to drift around her shoulders like a gold net veil.

'Oh, damn!' she exclaimed, impatiently grabbing her hair as if it was one of her most annoying features rather than one of her loveliest. 'Let me tie this back.'

'Leave it loose,' he said.

Ignoring him, she made short work of the repair. 'Smile,' she prompted, hearing the irritation in his voice. 'These wines are really good. You should be celebrating.'

It felt good to be like this with a woman—making some sort of real contact outside of bed and having her stand up to him for once.

'In fact, your wine's so good,' Grace went on, 'I'm going to forgive most of your transgressions.'

'I wasn't aware that I was guilty of any,' he said, warming even more to Grace.

'Well, I'm going to move on to the next part of my evaluation,' she said.

'Which is?' he said suspiciously.

'Drinking your health,' she said, disarming him.

They both reached for the same glass at the same time and their fingers touched. Grace snatched her hand away, as if she'd been burned, while his inner voice warned that he was playing a very dangerous game indeed if he wanted to send Grace home, because he could only wish that touch had lingered.

'This wine would benefit from being in storage a little longer,' she said, purely business—though she couldn't know his interest was now drawn to her lips. 'I can tell you now that we won't be ordering this one just yet. I'd like to taste it again next year.'

'Next year?' he repeated with amusement. 'You're very sure of yourself, Grace.'

'Why shouldn't I be?' she said. 'Do you think I'll have left Elias by then?'

He shrugged. 'I wouldn't know.'

Grace could be enigmatic when it suited her, and at other times be surprisingly frank. He wasn't used to mystery where women were concerned. He wasn't used to them holding out on him, either. But Grace was different. Other women had a straightforward agenda that dovetailed nicely with his. They communicated their messages with a glance—an option that wasn't open to Grace. Would she use that sort of tactic anyway? Grace was so forthright she was more likely to come straight out and tell him exactly what she wanted.

Could be interesting, he mused as he watched her roll the wine around her mouth.

'I need a moment,' she said, feeling for a space on the table to put her glass. 'I'd like to get some preparatory notes down. And while I'm doing that shall I e-mail Elias to warn him I shall be returning home tomorrow?'

No woman had ever presented him with a veiled threat before, and Grace had done so in such a clever way that he would have to think up some equally elegant punishment for her. He knew just the thing, and his senses roared as he thought about it.

'You mentioned seeing the wine in production,' he remarked, easing back from the table. 'So you can't leave tomorrow. I want that order, Grace. And there's an event I think you'd be interested in finding out more about.'

'Well, if you want me to stay...'

Clever girl, he thought, making it seem like his idea.

'I want you to finish the job,' he said. 'And I want a positive outcome.'

'Of course you do,' she agreed.

He wasn't ready to let Grace go yet, he realised, when he saw the corner of her mouth tip up. He wanted to know more about her. He wanted to know everything about her.

'What is this event?' she asked, distracting him.

'One of the wildest celebrations of the year—and extremely relevant,' he added in a serious tone, pulling his mind away from its stroll on the dark side.

'And you're sure it's important for me to know more about it?'

'Positive,' he said.

Teasing Grace was a delight, he decided as she reached for her laptop.

But as she took hold of it somehow she lost her grip, and as the computer slipped from her hands it sent bottles and wine glasses flying, spraying wine across the room.

'No harm done,' he said, snatching at Grace with one hand, to stop her falling, and her laptop with the other before it hit the floor.

'I feel such an idiot!' she exclaimed angrily.

'Nothing's damaged except your pride,' he pointed out, but as he settled everything back in place, including Grace, he noticed that she was close to tears.

Recovering fast, she sniffed noisily. 'Did I get you?' she said.

He ruffled his hair. 'Will it disappoint you too much if I say no?'

When she smiled his heart nearly exploded. He reached forward on impulse—to say something, to reassure her, maybe—but as Grace turned to look at him with a rueful expression on her face, and he knew she couldn't see him, a touch or an explanation of how he felt no longer seemed enough.

He leaned forward and kissed her instead. It was a crazy, impulsive thing to do—and more telling than he could have imagined.

'I'll get a cloth,' he said as she gasped, 'and some soda water,' he added, pulling back.

'Please don't worry,' she said tensely, feeling the extent of the damage with her hands. 'I can always soak my clothes overnight.'

Something inside him snapped. 'Do you always have to be so damned independent?' he exclaimed with frustration.

There was a pause, and then she said softly, 'Yes, I do.'

CHAPTER SIX

She'd made such a mess of everything. That was the only conclusion she could draw when she woke the next morning.

For a moment she couldn't move or think for her embarrassment. Her head was full of the wine flying everywhere and Nacho's consoling kiss. It was a gesture he might have made towards Lucia in one of his softer moments, and there had been nothing more said about it when he had brought her home. He'd simply seen her to the door and then left.

Grace's only consolation was that she knew she had done a good job with the wine. Elias was right. The Acosta vineyards were producing wine of exceptional quality now. The only question was, could they sustain it? What condition were the vineyards in, for instance. At least she could take some pleasure in knowing she had the edge over Nacho at the tasting. It could take ten years or more to become a master sommelier, but she had such a passion for the work she was getting there quicker than most. But that could never be uppermost in her mind now, because Nacho occupied *that* spot.

Swinging out of bed, she padded across the warm wooden floor in the direction of the open window, following the breeze. Opening the window a little more, she leaned over the sill to enjoy the sunshine. It was going to be a lovely day. She could smell the grass, its scent intensified by the dew, and the blossom that Nacho's housekeeper had explained twirled in big fat loops around the window. She dipped her fingers into the cool damp petals, enjoying both the feel of them and their scent.

She could smell horses too, Grace realised, raising her head. And hear them—along with a group of men's voices.

Conscious that she was only wearing pyjamas, she pulled back and stood to one side of the window, where she hoped she wouldn't be seen. Those older, gruffer voices must belong to the *gauchos* who worked with the horses. She smiled to think they must be herding ponies right past her bedroom window. What an experience! Wild Criollas from the pampas, she guessed. The noise was growing louder and dust was tickling her nose.

'I'd love to ride one,' she informed Buddy, who had come to snuggle at her legs, no doubt as keen as she was to explore outside.

The horses sounded like a crowd of naughty schoolchildren just set free for the holidays, Grace thought, listening hard for the distinctive prance of Nacho's stallion. But even without him this was kind of exciting, with the *gauchos* whooping and whistling as they rode past. If only she could see them…

The pain of loss almost doubled her over. She had been warned about this at the hospital, and though she knew that grieving for something that couldn't be changed was a pointless exercise it didn't stop it hurting.

She would just have to wait it out, Grace reasoned, biting hard on her lip. She refused to let it spoil her day.

A day without Nacho was already ruined, she reflected, wishing she could go home and forget all about this stupid mission.

But that was the last thing she really wanted to do, Grace realised, calming down. She had earned her right to be here, and she was going to stay until the job was done. She was going to take a shower and get dressed, and then she was going to take Buddy for his walk. She had always known that repairing the damage to her confidence when she'd lost her sight was never going to happen overnight. She just had to get used to these setbacks and accept that in the scheme of things two years was only a blink on her journey to recovery.

'Yes, I'm out riding,' he informed Lucia impatiently. 'I've been out since dawn. Why didn't you tell me about Grace? And don't tell me she asked you not to, because you're my sister and this is family.'

'And Grace is my friend,' Lucia fired back. 'And there is such a thing as loyalty to your friends, Nacho. Didn't *you* teach me that?' his sister added sharply. 'I don't know what all the fuss is about. Grace is making a great recovery, and I hate it when people treat her differently. I never thought *you* would.'

'I never said I had—'

'So what's your problem, Nacho? Why are you calling me in the middle of the night?'

'Is it?' he said, only now realising that with his head full of Grace he hadn't considered the time difference. 'Don't you have a baby to feed? What are you complaining about?'

'You're all heart, Nacho. Thanks to you, said baby is now wide awake and howling.'

'So go feed him,' he said as lusty screams threatened

to deafen them both. 'But before you go tell me more about Grace—'

'What do you want to know?' his sister demanded impatiently. 'That Grace is the bravest woman I know? That she copes with what's happened to her without complaint? I hope you're not being mean to her, Nacho. She needs our love—'

'*Your* love, maybe.'

'Just try and be kind to her, Nacho.'

'What do you take me for? I'm curious about her, that's all, and if I can't ask you—'

'If this is curiosity you've picked a strange time to call. Your interest in Grace sounds more like unfinished business to me.'

'*Dios*, Lucia. I hardly know the girl.'

'And you hardly want to take on more responsibility— which is how you must see it,' his sister said more gently.

'My interest in Grace is purely professional. I need to know if she can do the job or if I must call someone else.'

'Right,' Lucia agreed sarcastically. 'You usually canvas my opinion on a member of your staff in the middle of the night. How could I have forgotten that?'

'All I'm saying is, you could have warned me.'

'What?' Lucia snapped, all fired up now. 'That my *blind* best friend is now a sommelier, working for one of the most respected wine merchants in the world?'

'There's no need for you to be like that.'

'And there's no need for *you* to sound so prejudiced when I know you're not.'

'I didn't call you for a lecture, Lucia. As it happens, Grace did very well with the wine tasting, but how can she be expected to inspect a vineyard when she can't even *see* it?'

'I'm no expert, Nacho, but I think you should give

her a chance.' There was a pause, and then Lucia said, 'Grace has really got to you, hasn't she?'

He huffed an incredulous laugh. 'In twenty-four hours?'

'Is that how long you've been back?' Lucia exclaimed. 'If you hadn't told me I would have thought you and Grace had been together for months.'

'Goodbye, Lucia.'

'You'd better not hurt her, Nacho...'

'Who do you think you're talking to?'

'My uncompromising brother. Just don't ruin things before they have a chance to begin—'

'I can assure you that nothing's starting,' he cut in, and as the infant's wails reached a crescendo he judged it the perfect time to end the call.

Was he prejudiced against Grace?

No. He was a realist, Nacho concluded, loosening the reins to allow his stallion to pick its way downhill.

Could he work with Grace?

Of course not. But the annual grape-treading celebration *was* a valuable sales tool. She should not miss it. There weren't many vineyards left that stuck to the old ways, and in today's competitive market they needed all the differentials they could get. He was confident she'd be impressed. Each year at Viña Acosta a small amount of fruit was held back and processed in the old way. For luck, the old timers always said, and who was he to argue? It was good for morale, and everyone loved a party.

Now they were back on level ground he urged the stallion into a gallop. As he leaned low over the big horse's straining neck he wondered what Grace would make of such a high-octane event being used as an excuse for every type of excess. Would Grace loosen up and join in, or would she hold back and resist getting half-naked and drenched in juice?

He'd hold her back, he concluded as his senses roared. His imagination was enough to tell him that he couldn't possibly expose Grace to the sultry light of evening in the grape-treading vat, where everyone was wild and free. Grace, with her long blonde hair gleaming in the moonlight and her skin damp from her endeavors and sweet grape juice? Never…

Grace, her face flushed with anticipation as she moved into his arms…

She was here, he told himself impatiently, blanking the X-rated images from his mind as he straightened up and reined in, and Grace wanted research. He'd give her research. And, if he was looking for more excuses, escorting Grace to the celebration was the least he could do for Lucia's best friend while she was here.

Okay, she was going to be sensible. Well, most of the time. But when the darkness grew heavy and weighed her down she knew from bitter experience that the only way to rise up and find the light again was to do something different—something that really challenged her and took her mind off things. And she desperately wanted to ride a horse. She always had.

So what was stopping her? When would she get a chance like this again? What was the harm in asking? The head honcho could only say no, Grace reasoned as Buddy led her across the road towards the corral, where the men were talking. She couldn't hear Nacho's voice, so that was good. She wasn't going to make a complete fool of herself in front of him, and the banter between the men sounded good-natured.

'*Buenos Diás*,' she called out with a smile.

'*Buenos Días, señorita.* How may I help you?'

An older man was speaking, and what her shadowy vision couldn't see her mind supplied. He didn't stand too close, which she liked, and when he shifted positions she heard the chink of spurs. Her keen nose picked up the scent of tobacco and horse, along with leather and the smell of clean clothes dried in the sunshine. She could feel the older man's stare, steady on her face, and sensed it lacked opinion or censure. He was merely interested and friendly, and she thought he seemed kind.

'I'd like to ride a horse,' she said, coming right out with it. Angling her head, she put a wry expression on her face as she braced herself for refusal.

'No problem,' he said. 'Have you ever ridden a horse before?'

'A donkey at the seaside,' she admitted with a grin.

The elderly *gaucho* laughed at this. 'Then it will be my honour to teach you how to ride one of our gentle Criolla ponies, *señorita.*'

'Do you mean you're all right with it?'

'Why shouldn't I be?' he said.

Grace exhaled shakily. 'No reason at all,' she said.

He had just crested the hill when he saw Grace riding in the paddock. His heart took a leap as he quickly evaluated the risk at the scene. Having reassured himself that Alejandro, his head man, was riding shotgun alongside Grace, while Buddy rested patiently in the shade, he realised he hadn't felt so anxious for a long time.

He didn't slow his pace until he was close enough for Grace's pony to smell the stallion, at which point he reined in because he didn't want to spook it. Grace was concentrating, her mouth fixed in a determined line, as Alejandro issued instructions. As she squeezed her knees, urging the pony from a brisk walk to a bouncing trot, he grimaced, imagining that at any moment she might be thrown off.

Dismounting at speed, he lashed his reins to the fence.

'Nacho... Is that you?'

He felt a rush of pleasure, he was forced to admit, at the fact that Grace knew him immediately. 'You caught me out,' he said in a neutral tone. Alejandro had it all in hand, he realised, checking again. Propping one booted foot against the fence, he leaned his chin on folded arms and settled in to watch.

'Did you think you could stand there watching without me knowing?' she said, bouncing by.

'I thought I could try,' he admitted wryly.

'With a tread that's so distinctive I could never mistake it, and the snorts of your fire-breathing stallion to confirm what I already know? Yep, you could do that,' she teased him as she bounced past again.

The first thing he noticed was that she was smiling, and that she was radiant. 'You seem to be enjoying yourself,' he said.

'I am,' she enthused. 'Alejandro is such a wonderful teacher!'

He exchanged a look with his elderly friend. Alejandro shrugged as if to say, I was here—where were you?

'I want to ride *your* horse next,' Grace called out to him from the far side of the corral.

'In another universe,' he called back. 'My stallion's far too big for you.'

'No surprise there,' she said with a laugh in her voice. 'You could hardly be seen riding a donkey, now, could you?'

Alejandro laughed with Grace, and even Nacho's lips tugged in a smile. The events of last night hadn't dampened Grace's spirits, apparently. He liked her spirit. It was hard not to.

'Any chance we can get some work done today?' he said, removing his bandana to mop the dust from his face.

'The grapes aren't going anywhere, are they?' Grace demanded as he raked at his ungovernable hair. 'And why are you trying to change the subject, Nacho? What about the challenge of me riding your horse? Or are you frightened I might show you how easy it is in front of Alejandro?'

He laughed. 'You wish.'

'You could lead us, if you don't trust me not to gallop off with him. I'd love to try him, Nacho…'

'No,' he said firmly. 'Even my brothers are wary of this horse. He's not a tame pony like the one you're riding. He's still half wild.'

'Alejandro already explained that,' she butted in. 'He said your horse used to be the alpha male in a herd of Criollas until you tamed him.'

'Criollas can never be completely tamed. He still thinks he's the boss.'

'Still,' she said, 'I bet he'd be kind to *me*. Shall we find out?'

'Only I can ride him,' he said—with all the arrogance of which an Acosta brother was capable, Grace realised, keenly tuned in to the nuances in every voice.

'If that's the case,' she said innocently, 'the only way I can ever hope to ride him is with you.'

He laughed again. 'You must be joking—'

'What's your problem, Nacho? I realise the stallion is a mountain of muscle compared to me, while the pony I'm riding now is…' she shrugged and pressed her lips together in a teasing, slanting smile '…also a mountain of muscle compared to me.'

Alejandro shot Nacho a sympathetic look before vaulting the fence and leaving him to it. The wily old stockman had left him with no option but to look after Grace. 'You're not even dressed for riding,' he remarked disapprovingly.

'Oh, come on, Nacho,' she goaded him.

Grace was half his size, and slender as a willow. She was wearing a long, floating dress that couldn't have been more unsuitable for riding if she'd tried, and only now he noticed she was barefoot.

And she was blind.

Grace Lundström was the most aggravating woman he had ever known—so perhaps it was time to show her the consequences of biting off more than she could chew.

'Alejandro,' he yelled, before the old *gaucho* disappeared. 'Can you look after the dog for us?'

'*Sí*, Señor Acosta,' Alejandro replied, in an amused voice that prompted Nacho to narrow his eyes.

He turned back to Grace. 'I'm prepared to take you for a short walk along the riverbank.'

'That's very kind of you,' she said—a little too sweetly for his liking.

'But if you're going to ride with me you do things *my* way,' he warned. 'Stay where you are. I'm going to help you dismount.'

'*Sí*, Señor Acosta,' she said, in a perfect take-off of Alejandro's mocking voice.

CHAPTER SEVEN

SERIOUSLY terrified at the thought of riding Nacho's horse, she was still serious about going ahead with it—if only to prove to herself that she could. Plus this was the ideal opportunity for her to prove to Nacho that being blind didn't put a curb on what she could do.

For once she obeyed him, and remained motionless in the pony's saddle until she felt the brush of his hands as he took hold of her reins. Even that brief contact was enough to send heat ripping up and down her spine in yet another reminder that the one mistake she was making was to think she could remain immune to the stallion's master.

'Don't move until I tell you to move,' Nacho instructed, 'and then you must do exactly as I say.'

'Yes, sir.'

'If you can't take this seriously—'

'But I am taking this very seriously, indeed,' Grace protested.

'I said *wait*,' he ground out as she slipped her feet out of the stirrups. 'I'll lift you clear. And don't kick the horse on your way down.'

'If I could see him—'

'I'll be your eyes. Now, slide into my arms,' Nacho instructed, without a moment wasted on pity or scorn.

Her heart was hammering nineteen to the dozen, which made her think that this was one time when not being able to see was a distinct advantage. Launching herself into the unknown, she found herself in Nacho's arms.

Whatever she'd imagined it might feel like, she'd been wrong. Her imagination was in no way equal to the task. Sliding down such a wealth of muscle was like nothing else on earth, added to which Nacho's handprints were now branded on her body. And, yes, it would be safer to concentrate on more mundane things, like business, but mundane things were a little short on the ground right now, and all she was aware of was Nacho throwing off testosterone like a Catherine wheel threw off sparks.

'Steady,' he murmured.

'Me or the horse?'

She gasped when he caught her round the waist, and the next thing she knew she was airborne.

'I'm lowering you gently into the saddle in front of me,' Nacho explained. 'So we don't give the horse a shock.'

What about *her* shock?

As if her swift rise into thin air hadn't been alarming enough, she now had her buttocks rammed up hard against Nacho. Fighting the urge to arch her back and feel more of that hard body against hers was the least of her worries. Nacho had somehow swept her skirt back as he lifted her, so now she was sitting astride his horse with her dress rucked up to her knickers and her confidence evaporating rapidly.

'I thought you were going to lead me along the riverbank,' she protested.

'You thought wrong,' he said, and with a click of his tongue against the roof of his mouth they were off.

At the stallion's first surge forward she was sure she would crash to the ground. She had never felt that much power beneath her before, and not knowing how far she had to fall made each rolling step the horse took absolutely terrifying.

'Are you okay, Grace?' Nacho demanded, tightening his grip on her.

'I think so...' Her voice sounded small and feeble, and he must have felt her tension, but it wasn't just fear of falling that had turned her into such a coward. It was Nacho's primitive energy that seemed to be throbbing through both of them.

She could feel his heart thudding against her back, slow and strong, and his hard muscles shifting behind her. The warmth of his body against hers was intimate beyond anything she could imagine. She sat forward a little, to put some distance between them. For all his wealth and polish Nacho exuded an earthy, animalistic quality that made her ultra-aware of him. She could understand now why women wanted to go to bed with him and why men feared him.

And no one with any sense got this close to danger without expecting to get burned.

Her inner voice of caution might advise that, but clearly she had no sense, Grace concluded, because she was starting to enjoy the sensation. And, as far as the riding went, she was determined to make a go of it.

'What do you need me to do?'

'As little as possible,' Nacho said. 'Just relax. If you tense up the horse will feel it and become restless. You have to go with me—move with me.'

Really...?

With her back to him she was free to smile, and then, concentrating, she tried again.

'That's better,' Nacho approved when she started to get the hang of it.

Grace's legs were slender as a newborn fawn's, but there was nothing weak or unsteady about her. There was a line between weakness and fragility, and no one would ever mistake Grace for being weak. His mother had been weak. He could see that now. Though nothing excused what he had done. He had never turned his back on anyone before or since the fateful day of the tragedy, and he never would again.

'Is this right?' Grace asked, jolting him back to the present.

'Just about perfect,' he confirmed.

She was riding really well, but then no one could ever accuse Grace of shirking a challenge. He could see now that since her illness she had worked hard to prove herself. She had retrained and learned all sorts of new skills. She had proved herself at the wine tasting, and again with his *gauchos*, and now she had somehow talked him into letting her ride his best horse. Perhaps most surprising of all was the way the big stallion was picking his route with more care than usual, as if he knew he had precious cargo on board.

If his brothers could only see this, Nacho reflected with amusement.

'Riding is even more fun than I thought!' Grace exclaimed.

He felt the now customary bolt of shock and pain when she turned her lovely face his way and her gaze flew somewhere to the right of his face.

'There's so much power beneath us,' she enthused. 'This is just wonderful, Nacho.'

Even as he warmed inside he remembered the harm he could do to those he cared about. 'Sit straight,' he rapped, mentally pulling back to concentrate on the practicalities of teaching Grace to ride. 'You shouldn't be looking at me. You should be looking forward, between the horse's ears.'

'If I could *look* anywhere,' she corrected him humorously.

Vicious curses invaded his head. 'Sorry—'

'Don't be,' she said. 'Riding is too much fun for us to worry about anything. Who cares?'

That Grace had lost her sight? He did. 'Feel for his ears, Grace. Good. Now, that's where you should be pointing your nose.'

She started to laugh. 'Are you saying I've got a big nose?'

She had a perfect nose. 'Line up your body,' he instructed. 'Not stiffly like that,' he complained with an impatient sigh. 'Draw yourself up and relax into his gait. That's better. Allow your hips to move easily back and forth in rhythm with his stride. Good. Well done, Grace.' She was a natural. 'Did anyone else ever take you riding?' he asked, feeling a stab at the thought that there might be someone in her past who had done so.

'A man once,' she mused, leaning back against him as she appeared to think about it.

'What man?' he said angrily, moving away.

'A man at the seaside.'

'The seaside?' he cut in suspiciously, as visions of sun-drenched beaches and handsome polo players on half-wild ponies sprang to mind.

'The man at the seaside who ran a team of donkeys,' she said.

'Are you teasing me?'

'Maybe,' she admitted, and there was a smile in her voice.

He was relieved. There was no getting away from it. He was very much relieved.

Clicking his tongue against the roof of his mouth, he urged the stallion on—which gave him every excuse to hold Grace more firmly. 'Trust me,' he said as she grabbed a hank of mane. 'You're safe with me, Grace.'

Safe with Nacho? Was he mad? Was *she* mad, for that matter? And a ragdoll pegged out in a gale would have more poise than she had right now. She was bumping up and down on the saddle like a sack of potatoes.

'I'm going to help you to move correctly, Grace.'

Thank goodness he couldn't see the expression on her face now, she thought.

'You're not frightened, are you?' he said, feeling her tension.

'No,' she protested. But she was. She was frightened of the way Nacho made her feel…his touch on her body, his breath on her skin; the way she felt so safe, cocooned in the warmth of his arms. She could so easily get used to this—and that would only end in heartbreak.

At Lucia's wedding, when Nacho had singled her out, her head had started spinning with wild, romantic nonsense. In the cool light of day she had realised it was pure nonsense without any of the romance. And now Nacho was only being kind to his sister's blind friend. She shouldn't read anything more into this riding lesson.

'You're doing really well,' he said, loosening his grip. 'You're on your own now, Grace.'

'What?' she exclaimed, a bolt of terror running through her. 'I'm not ready to go it alone.'

Nacho said nothing; he just let her go, which was really scary in her darkness. She just had to trust he wouldn't let her fall.

It was completely unnerving at first, but she was so

determined to do it that gradually she found her balance, and once she'd done that she started enjoying herself. Turning her face to the sun, she sighed with pleasure.

'Buddy's come to join us,' Nacho remarked. 'Shall we give him a run?'

'Oh, please,' she agreed, sitting up straight again. 'Let's go faster.'

The speed, the wind in her hair, cantering across the countryside with Nacho—all of it was exhilarating. And also a pointed reminder that she was a novice where so much in life was concerned, while Nacho was notoriously the master of all things with risk attached. She was sexually inexperienced. He was not. Yes, she'd had a few attempts at relationships, but had never seen what all the fuss was about. And there had been piano practice in her young life, followed by hard work when she was older, leaving barely any time to spare for thoughts of romance.

But she could think about romance now. With the stallion's hooves pounding beneath her it was impossible to think of anything *but* romance. She could be galloping across the desert with a sheikh, or riding into the sunset with a cowboy. Or, better still, Grace concluded, smiling to herself, she could be riding across the pampas with Nacho.

He had nudged the horse into an easy canter, knowing the swaying rhythm would be easier for Grace to handle than a high-stepping trot. And it was. But with Grace pressed up against him and all that power harnessed beneath them there was fever in his blood.

'Work your hips back and forth,' he said, trying to concentrate on teaching Grace to ride. 'You need to loosen up, Grace.'

She took him at his word and leaned her head against

his chest in a gesture that was both intimate and trusting, surprising him again.

'Is Buddy okay?' she said, sitting up just as he was getting used to having her resting against him.

'He's fine.' Reining in, he slowed the stallion to a walking pace. 'Did Alejandro mention the grape-treading to you tonight?'

'He did say something about a party,' she admitted. 'He also said he hoped I'd be there. But I suppose I'd need an invitation for that...'

He laughed. 'Stop fishing, Grace. You know you've got one.'

'I know why,' she said. 'You're hoping I might use the event in our forward publicity if Elias decides to go ahead and place an order.' She laughed. 'But if you think my attendance tonight guarantees that order, think again. I've got a lot more to see.'

'Are you playing hardball with me, Señorita Lundström? Because if you are I shall have to frighten you into submission. Are you ready for more speed?'

'Try me,' she said. 'You don't frighten me, Señor Acosta.'

As she spoke she turned, and as she turned his gaze slipped to her lips. 'At least allow me to try,' he murmured.

He had to admire Grace when the stallion bounded forward and she started whooping with excitement. 'Does nothing frighten you?' he called against the wind blowing in their faces.

'Only the darkness,' she yelled back, making him rage inwardly against the cruel fate that had left her blind.

He reined in at the guest cottage, where he told Grace to wait while he dismounted so he could help her down. But, as he might have known, she didn't wait and somehow managed to slip to the ground without his help, only staggering slightly as she regained her balance.

'Thank you,' she said formally, holding out her hand for him to shake. 'That was wonderful, Nacho. And now I've taken up enough of your time.'

She was dismissing him. 'Alejandro has hung Buddy's harness on the fence,' he said. 'It's over there to your right—'

'No use pointing, Nacho.'

'Grace, I—'

'I know. You're sorry.'

'Hanging from the main post,' he explained patiently.

'What time will you call for me tonight?' she said, finding the harness.

'Same time as last night.'

'Fine by me,' she said. 'Thanks again for the riding lesson.'

'There's just one thing.'

'Which is?'

'Buddy can't come tonight.'

'That's okay,' she said with a shrug. 'I was expecting it.'

'Until tonight, Grace...' He vaulted into the saddle.

'Until tonight,' she said, turning for the door.

Being without Buddy for one night wouldn't be a problem, Grace reflected as she let herself into the house. Even back home there were some places he couldn't go. She kept the hated stick for those occasions. It was collapsible, and fitted in a suitcase, which was about the best that could be said for it...

Nacho hadn't gone yet. She could hear his horse snorting and stamping. Nacho must be watching her. It made her nervous.

As she took the key out of the lock she stepped back

and almost tripped over Buddy. She swore like a trooper and then heard Nacho laugh. 'All right for you,' she called out.

'*Dios,* Grace,' he shot back, 'I thought you were so well behaved, but now I realise it must have been you who led my sister astray.'

She laughed. 'Sussed. Decorum was never my strong point. Talking of which—what do I wear tonight?'

Nothing would be his preference. 'I'll speak to someone,' he said, 'and I'll have some suitable clothes delivered to the cottage for you to wear.'

'Really?' she called excitedly. 'Great.'

The thought of Grace in traditional clothes suitable for the grape-treading gave him quite a buzz as he rode back to the *hacienda.* He reflected on the day's events. How it had made him feel having Grace pressed up close against him on the horse. How it would feel tonight, escorting her to the grape-treading. Had he lost it completely, inviting her? Yes, it was a good research opportunity for Grace, but it would be a lot more than she'd bargained for. The annual wine-fest was hardly a sedate affair. Treading the grapes dated from antiquity—pagan times, before civilisation came along to spoil the fun and dictate restraint. It wasn't unusual for the next working day to start at noon, if at all—and those who arrived alone invariably left in pairs.

And now his big horse had bolted and it was his turn to swear. Sensing his abstraction, the mighty stallion had lost no time heading towards the hills and freedom. Wrestling him back under control was a welcome outlet for his energy, but it did nothing to soothe his thoughts. Grace liked teasing him, but then she drew back. She craved independence. Well, she could have it—with his blessing. She would just have to take her chances with the men at the grape-treading.

Are you seriously advocating open season where Grace is concerned?

He wouldn't let her out of his sight tonight.

It was safe to say that the outfit which had arrived at the cottage didn't conform to Grace's usual take on a party outfit. That would be more likely to consist of a knee-length shift in silk or wool, depending on the weather, and safe, low-heeled shoes. But this wasn't a usual party, Grace reflected as she sorted out the clothes by touch. Though 'grape-treading' was probably an old term, used loosely these days to describe what happened to the fruit at the start of wine production, she decided.

She tried on the skirt first. Masses of fabric brushed her calves, making her feel like a country girl in an oil painting. The blouse was flimsy, and it had lace around the generous neckline—which would slip straight off her sloping shoulders. She held it to her face and inhaled the scent of soap and sunshine. As to colour? White was her best guess. The blouse was also cut low across the bust, and fastened with laces rather than buttons.

What would Nacho think of the transformation? Grace wondered as she slipped on her sandals. She should pin her hair up—though that would leave her shoulders bare…

And now it was too late to change. The clock had just struck six. Time for business. With no way of knowing what she looked like, she smoothed the full skirt anxiously. Should she have worn a bra? It was a bit late to be worrying about that now, she concluded, brushing her nipples lightly with the palm of her hands to see

if the cotton fabric was thick enough to conceal them.
Probably not…

She jumped as Buddy barked. It was too late to change
her clothes *or* her mind. She would just have to brace
herself and go through with it. She opened the door.

'Grace—'

Why the sudden silence? Did she look ridiculous? Was
she wearing everything the right way round? Had she
forgotten to tie the laces on her blouse? She checked discreetly as she invited Nacho to come in. The air swirled
as he walked past, and her body responded to the pure
zap of Nacho's energy like a teenager on her first date.
She drank greedily on the aroma of citrus soap, mint
toothpaste and hot, hard man. There was a lot of heat—
and quite a bit of it on her cheeks.

'You'd better tell me if I look okay,' she said, closing
the door behind him.

There was a long pause, and then he said, 'You look
great.'

Great was a major understatement. Grace looked
amazing in the revealing top and traditional skirt. Her
breasts were magnificent. He would definitely have to
watch the other men tonight. He might be duty bound to
maintain cordial relations with his sister and keep Elias
onside, but tonight Grace belonged to *him*.

'Will I fit in at the wine-treading?' she asked him.

No, you'll stand out because you look so beautiful,
he thought. 'You'll do,' he said casually. Her skin was
luminous, and flushed from riding in the sun, and her
hair was gleaming with good health. If he could find
fault it was that she'd put her hair up. But as there was
only one pin holding it…

'Describe your outfit,' she said, distracting him. 'I

want to make sure I'm not the only one dressed up like a marionette.'

Some puppet show, he thought. And then, while he was thinking how beautiful she looked, she hit him with a zinger.

'I need to feel you,' she said.

'I beg your pardon?'

'I need to feel you so I know what you're wearing,' she said. 'It's how I see now.'

'Don't you trust me to tell you?'

'What do you think?' she said.

She advanced hands outstretched.

'All right, go ahead,' he said with a shrug, lifting his arms.

She started with his face. 'You haven't shaved.'

'I wasn't planning on kissing anyone tonight.'

Her cheeks flushed red. 'I should think not. I've no intention of being a gooseberry.'

He thought she might have had enough of the game by now, but no.

'You're wearing jeans,' she said, brushing his thighs with the lightest of touches. And then she exclaimed with fright as her hands touched naked skin.

CHAPTER EIGHT

'I CHOPPED my jeans off above the knee,' he explained. 'It's easier than rolling them up.'

'You might have warned me.' Her hands moved deftly on, sadly missing any interesting parts of his anatomy. 'You needn't hold your breath,' she said.

'I don't know what you mean,' he defended wryly.

'I think I just got scorched by your affront,' she remarked. 'I'm sure you've got a six-pack at the very least.'

'At the very least,' he agreed.

She mapped the width of his chest and seemed satisfied as she stood back. 'You're wearing a casual shirt,' she said. 'Describe it.'

'Dark blue—a little frayed, a little faded.'

'And you still have tattoos?'

'Of course.'

'The Band of Brothers—I remember,' she said, returning to her investigations. Her little hand didn't make it halfway round his upper arm. 'And I seem to remember something inked in black on this big muscle here...'

'You saw my tattoos during that polo match on the beach?' Should he be quite so pleased she had remembered? 'How much can you see now, Grace?' he enquired, as curiosity got the better of him.

She laughed. 'Enough to know that you block out the light.'

She must be mad. What was she doing, feeling her way around Nacho? She would never have dreamed of doing anything so intimate when she could see—so why now, when she was blind?

There had to be some advantages to being blind, she reasoned.

'I can see fuzzy shapes,' she revealed, in the interest of much needed distraction. 'If the light's good and I lift my chin I can see…' *The vaguest outline of your sexy mouth…* 'Vague shapes,' she said, keeping as close as possible to the truth.

'Is that it?' he said.

'Not yet. Stand still,' she chided when he moved. She was beginning to enjoy this, though her heart was still thundering off the scale. 'I'm glad you remembered your bandana,' she said as she traced the band across his brow. 'Wild hair must be contained at all times, according to health and safety rules,' she teased.

'Don't forget the earring and the scowl.'

Forget safety, Grace thought, hearing the humour in Nacho's voice. 'You're not scowling,' she said.

Nacho laughed.

This was not going the way he had imagined. He had come to the cottage with a clear plan in his mind. This was not a date. He would be polite to Grace—chivalrous, even. He would escort her to the grape-treading, where he would keep her safe and help her to do her research. And that was it. If he'd known she was going to explore him so thoroughly with her hands he might have made different plans—like taking her to bed and to hell with the grape-treading, along with his guilty past and all his worthy resolutions.

'Are we ready?' Grace asked as she walked to the door.

He didn't know about her, but he was ready enough to be in agony. 'What? No laptop, notebook, or phone to take notes?'

'None of the above,' she said. 'Tonight is strictly for enjoyment—I'll learn more that way,' she insisted.

'So what did Alejandro tell you about tonight?'

'He told me to be careful around you,' she said.

'Me?' When she laughed he thought he'd have to have a word with Alejandro.

Swinging the door wide, he realised Grace wasn't with him, and felt a punch in the guts when he turned to see her feeling for a stick. It was so easy to forget there was anything wrong with Grace.

'Locking this thing into place is a real pain,' she complained good-humouredly as she wrestled with the stick's extension lever. 'It collapses, so that's good, because I can pack it in my suitcase, but just try and get the damn thing to stay fixed in place.'

'You won't need it,' he said. Taking the stick away from Grace, he propped it against the wall. 'You've got me tonight,' he reminded her.

The barn where the grape-treading was being held was already full of people. He drew Grace close to protect her from the crowd. She felt tiny against him, but she felt full of energy too. Her curiosity was firing on all cylinders, he realised when he stared down into her face.

'Describe the scene to me,' she said.

As he looked around him he realised that he was noticing so much more. He'd never paid so much attention to his surroundings in his life, but that had been before Grace had come to Argentina and now he absolutely had to.

'Well, the barn is packed,' he began.

'I can feel that—and I can hear it,' she said, laughing. She clung to him as they moved through the crowd. 'You'll have to do better than that, Nacho.'

So he, who never fell short in anything, according to popular belief, was forced to try again. But just for now he wanted to absorb the feeling of being close to Grace—protecting her. He had never been so physically close to a woman outside of bed, and this was far better. Grace was almost a friend. She was certainly a very special business associate. He kept her pressed up hard against him—for reasons of safety only, of course.

'I hope you're not isolating me, Nacho?'

'Isolating you?'

'Only it's quieter here, and I'm not being jostled. I don't want to be regarded as an oddity,' she exclaimed. 'And I don't want you making special allowances for me.'

'What if they're steering a wide berth around *me*?' he said.

'Are you so fearsome?' She huffed with disbelief. 'I don't think so. From talking to Alejandro I get the sense that your staff really like and respect you. And, as you're taking time out from your crazy overloaded schedule to revive their industry, I can only think they must really admire you too.'

'Maybe I am being a little over-protective,' he conceded, loosening his grip. Habit of a lifetime, he reflected.

'That's better,' she said. 'Now we can both relax and enjoy the party. So long as you describe it to me...'

He was keen to do that. He didn't want her to miss out on anything. 'We're in a big all-purpose barn, constructed from old, mellow wood, I guess it's a sort of rich golden-brown—'

'High ceiling?'

'Very high,' he confirmed. 'With a pitched roof. The air is—'

'Warm, noisy, boisterous, and scented with old wine and anticipation,' she said, her face illuminated with the eagerness of a child as she raised her chin. 'Go on—'

'I was about to say the air smells of dry hay and it's full of dust motes.'

'Romantic.'

'Do you want me to describe it to you or not?'

'You dare stop. It gives me a lovely warm feeling inside when you describe things. I just think you could use a few more adjectives.'

'Take it or leave it, Grace.'

'I'll take it, thank you,' she said, grinning up at him.

He smiled too, and dragged her a little closer. There was something so innately good in Grace it made him want to know more about her, and at the same time made him wonder if he would spoil his time with her as he had spoiled so many other things. Would the past haunt him until he had?

'Come on,' she prompted, 'I'm waiting...'

He reordered his mind. 'Most people are dressed in traditional clothes,' he explained, determined that Grace wouldn't miss out on anything. 'The older women are dressed in black, and some of the older men have big hats on—'

'And belts with coins dangling from them?' she said.

'How did you know that?'

'Because they're *gauchos*,' she said, as Lucia might. 'This isn't just a celebration for the people who work at the vineyard, is it? It's for everyone who works for you.'

'And anywhere the Acostas are you'll find a horse,' he confirmed.

She laughed. 'I was about to say that.'

They were guessing each other's sentences now.

'Are we anywhere near the grape-treading yet, Nacho?'

'I'm just getting you out of the way of it so that you don't get trampled in the rush.'

'I don't understand,' she said, sounding concerned.

'Don't worry. When the grape-treading starts we'll have front row seats.'

'Do you mean we won't be taking part? No,' she said emphatically. 'I have to do it. How can I possibly report on the grape-treading if I don't?'

'It will be too rough for you, Grace.'

'Nothing's too rough for me,' she insisted. 'And I don't know how you can even say that when *you're* here.'

'You'll be able to hear everything that's going on. I promise you.'

'That sounds like fun,' she said in a flat tone.

'What do you want me to do?' he said. 'Risk you getting trampled?'

'No,' she said. 'Why don't you take me back and lock me away in the cottage, where I'll be safe.'

'Grace—you can't.'

'Why can't I?' There was a pause, and then she said in a soft, angry voice, 'Don't you *dare*...'

He could come up with a whole raft of reasons why a blind woman couldn't take part in the grape-treading, including the fact that Grace could slip and fall, or could be jostled and hurt herself. But she was right. *He* was the coward, fearing something might happen to her and allowing the past to throw up obstacles—like the fear that he couldn't keep those he cared about safe. Grace was strong. She could do anything she set her mind to.

He shouldn't even think of stopping her when he would be there in the vat to protect her.

'Of course you can do it,' he agreed.

'No surrender?' she said fiercely.

'No surrender,' he agreed wryly.

'Like a sheep?' she said. 'So long as that's the worst I have to do.' She laughed as he led her forward.

He had to ask himself if he had ever felt such pleasure in a woman's company before. With most women everything was simply a prelude to bed, but with Grace there was so much more to learn—just being with her felt like a privilege, a gift.

'What's that sound?' she said, shrinking back in alarm.

'That's the sound of the grapes being tipped into the vat,' he explained. It went on and on, but he could see that now she knew what was invading her darkness Grace wasn't frightened any more. She laughed when he told her she would be up to her thighs in grapes inside the vat.

'Which means they'll probably be round *your* ankles,' she commented.

He asked himself again: was taking Grace into the vat sensible? He had noticed several of the local youths eyeing her up, and once they were inside the vat there would be no quarter given and no attention paid to status or rank. He was the acknowledged leader of the pack, but tonight there would be challenges to his supremacy. He had seen it in the eyes of the other men when they looked at Grace—not because she was blind, but because she was beautiful, and because she was with *him*. Combat was in their blood as much as it was in his. Claiming Grace wasn't so much a rational decision as a primitive compulsion. Those youths would stay away from her if they knew what was good for them.

A young woman showed Grace how to tuck up her skirt. She sounded friendly and kind, and Grace thanked her for her help. She was getting better at that, Grace realised. She wasn't always pushing people away now, as she had done initially, when she had first lost her sight. She'd also eased up a lot since she'd been in Argentina. Being with Nacho had done that. He was so no-nonsense he had unlocked something inside her. It was something that said everyone needed help sometimes and that it had nothing to do with pity. Nice people liked to help their fellow man, whatever their physical status might be. It had nothing to do with being blind.

'Do I look okay?' she asked, smoothing her hands over her naked thighs, feeling a bit self-conscious now.

'You look great,' he said.

The hint of a smile in his voice made her feel womanly and sexy for the first time in ages.

'Stay close to me, Grace.'

As if she had any option—as if she *wanted* one, Grace thought as Nacho put his arm around her shoulders and drew her close. He made her feel so safe.

'I'm going to lift you into the vat,' he said, making her heart race even faster. 'Wait there for me—I'll get in first.'

She listened intently when Nacho left her side and heard him vault over the side of the vat. There was a wet, squelching sound when he landed.

'Reach out—let me guide your hands,' he said.

Before she knew it she was over the side and knee-deep in grapes.

'How does that feel, Grace?'

'Wet!' she said.

Nacho laughed. 'Hold on to me so you don't fall.'

Well, *that* was no problem.

And then the band started to play, and as the tempo increased the crowd all around them began to jump rhythmically in the vat.

'This is seriously crazy,' she yelled, hanging on to Nacho for dear life. 'Don't you dare let me go!'

'Not a chance,' he husked in her ear.

She was soon stamping furiously like everyone else. She had never felt so abandoned and free. Her legs were swimming in warm juice and the sensation was erotic and amazing. Nacho should have warned her—but would she have come if he had?

As Nacho let go of her for a moment, to tug off his juice-drenched shirt, she realised her own blouse was soaked through with juice. She could only imagine how transparent it must be. And now her overly sensitive hands were free to roam Nacho's warm, naked skin. She could feel a wealth of muscle beneath her fingertips, and his heart throbbing strongly in his chest.

'You'll fall if you don't hold on,' he warned when she quickly drew her hands away.

She'd fall if she did, Grace thought.

He'd seen the other men looking at Grace with hunger in their eyes, and he felt his power surge even higher as she clung to *him*. He had left the other men in no doubt that he was the one Grace trusted to keep her safe.

The music stopped as suddenly as it had begun and a hush fell over the crowd. He knew what would happen next—though Grace had no idea why he was suddenly holding her so firmly. A few seconds passed, and then a drum began to beat. The sound was little more than a seductive whisper to begin with, but then it grew louder and faster, until everyone was stamping their feet to the same heated rhythm, and the air was charged with a primal energy that made his own senses sharpen in response.

More and more couples were leaving the vat, Grace noticed. There was a lot more room for manoeuvre, and not half so much yelling and laughter.

'I'll need at least an hour in the shower after this,' she told Nacho, laughing. The evening was coming to an end and she was reluctant to leave. Something had changed between them. Barriers had come down. Though she guessed she looked an incredible mess. She was sticky with juice, and without Buddy or her stick she had no alternative but to rely on Nacho to take her back home. 'But I don't want to spoil the evening for you,' she insisted. 'Why don't you come back to the party after you've walked me home?'

'Why would I do that?' he said. 'Come on, Grace. We're leaving.'

She liked that he made no fuss. Nacho just swung her into his arms and lifted her over the side of the vat. Then somehow he was there to steady her on the other side. She paused to straighten her skirt while Nacho found her sandals, but as he began to lead her away she felt disorientated. 'Where are we going?'

A wooden door creaked open in front of her and cool air hit her face. They were outside and away from everyone, with cobbles beneath their feet. And now they were crossing an open space that had to be big because all sound was lost on the wind.

'Where is this?' she said. 'A hay barn?' she guessed as Nacho opened another door. 'What are we doing here?'

'Even *you* can't be so naïve,' Nacho murmured.

CHAPTER NINE

LACING his fingers through her hair, Nacho cupped the back of her head in a way that was both possessive and achingly tender. The brush of his lips against hers was a remembered pleasure—though so much better now she was full of suppressed heat and longing.

She could feel his power flooding through her, mixing with her own to create some new, stronger force. When he tightened his grip, pressing insistently and hungrily against her, she kissed him back with an answering hunger that found its voice deep in her throat. Teasing her lips apart, he deepened the kiss and, finding her tongue with his, stroked it in a way that made intimate pulses throb deep between her thighs.

She moved against him, wanting more…more pleasure…more incredible sensation. Her mind blazed with a fever that no amount of reason could wipe out. She wanted him. And, impossibly, it appeared Nacho wanted her too.

'Where are you taking me?' she gasped as he swung her into his arms. She still felt that frisson of uncertainty, and wished beyond anything that she could see.

She had to trust him, Grace realised as Nacho soothed her with husky words in Spanish. She knew something of this man now, and she had to trust him to keep her safe.

Shouldering open another door, he let it bang shut behind them. 'I'm taking you to the *hacienda*.'

'To the *hacienda*?' she said.

'And then to bed.'

'And Buddy?'

'I'll make a call.'

Reassured, and yet terrified, she clung to Nacho as he strode across gravel and cobbles, and finally onto an even path. Another door swung wide, and they were inside again, somewhere quiet and calm and warm, where a clock was ticking reassuringly. She heard marble tiles beneath his feet and then a wide expanse of rug. They were inside the *hacienda* in a big hallway, Grace realised as Nacho turned and bounded up a flight of stairs. A *grand* staircase, she registered as they went up and up.

Trust Nacho to have his eyrie at the top of the house, she mused when they reached a thickly carpeted landing. He strode straight on and another door opened. Greeted by the scent of clean linen and beeswax, she guessed this was his bedroom.

The room was big. It ate up several of his strides before Nacho put her down on the bed. The windows were open, and she could feel the breeze and hear the swish of voile billowing.

She heard him switch a light on and smiled. 'I don't need the light,' she said.

'But I do,' Nacho argued, lying down at her side. 'I want to look at you.'

She remained still on sheets scented with lavender and sunshine, her head resting comfortably on a soft bank of pillows. She was trembling with awareness, Grace realised, waiting for Nacho to touch her or to speak.

Grace was the most beautiful thing he had ever seen. He marvelled that someone so tiny and vulnerable could be so strong. She was all he remembered from the wedding and so much more. He smiled to think she looked even better for being flushed and dishevelled after the grape-treading. Her hair had tumbled down and was wild around her shoulders, while the juice-stained blouse did nothing to conceal the full swell of her breasts. Grape juice streaked her cheek and her neck.

Bringing her into his arms, he kissed it away. She laughed against his mouth, and her laugh was the sexiest thing he had ever heard.

'Don't,' she said.

'Don't what?' He pulled his head back to look at her.

'Don't treat me as if I'm made of cut glass,' she warned him. 'I'm a woman like any other, Nacho.'

Not like any other, he thought. His hungry gaze swept Grace's body to find the cotton skirt had wrapped itself around her legs, exposing her elegant thighs. He thought of them spread wide and her legs locked around him… He wanted them joined deep. Moving over her, he teased her, with the weight of his thigh for the pleasure of hearing her groan. Taking his leg higher, he pressed more firmly, rubbing and teasing until she was gasping for breath.

'Don't—don't stop,' she said. Balling her hands, she pressed angry fists against his chest. 'There's nothing wrong with me. *Nothing*. Do you understand?'

'All I understand is that I want you,' he murmured, staring down. 'But what do *you* want, Grace?'

'You,' she said fiercely. 'I want you. I don't want you to see a blind woman,' she added in a voice that tore at his heart. 'I want you to see *me*. I want you to see Grace—'

'I always have,' he whispered, dragging her close.

And it was the truth. After that first terrible shock

he had come to see past the changes in Grace to everything that remained the same, and so much that had
grown stronger.

'There's no rush. We've got all night, Grace.'

'And this could take hours, I hope?'

He felt her smile against his mouth. 'At least…'

Happy with his answer, she laughed, and his hunger
spiked higher, driving back the ghosts from the past.

She had dreamed of this moment since she first saw
Nacho, but never in her wildest dreams had she imagined they would ever be together like this, or that she
could have the freedom of his body as he had hers. Nacho
had aroused her beyond the point of reason just with his
touch, and with the outrageous suggestions he was murmuring in her ear. He was the master of all things sensual, and he had made her want him with a hunger so
fierce it frightened her.

'Enough,' she complained. 'Stop teasing me.' She
writhed impatiently beneath him. 'Please don't make
me wait.'

But Nacho refused to be hurried, and was content to
leave her to imagine what might happen next.

'Please don't do this,' she begged in a shaking voice.

His answer was to tease her with his torso, brushing
his warm body against her until her nipples were on fire
and she was arcing against him, shamelessly seeking
contact. When he finally dipped his head to suckle her
nipples through the fine fabric of her blouse she uttered
a cry of sheer relief. But it wasn't enough. The pulse
between her legs was growing ever more demanding.
Every time she inhaled she drew in more of Nacho's in-
toxicating scent, and the thought of all his power, so ef-
fortlessly controlled and so completely at her disposal,
was more aphrodisiac than she could handle.

He had to curb Grace or it would all be over for her too soon. He had never anticipated this level of hunger, and wondered if he had ever seen anyone so aroused so quickly or so fiercely. Grace was like a lioness fighting for her mate, and it took all his skill to stroke and soothe and make her hold back. When she was quiet again he kissed her tenderly, but even then she couldn't stay still for long. Holding both her wrists, he pinned her on the bank of pillows. He was going to make this good for her. He was going to make this perfect.

He could never have anticipated that the solution to holding Grace back would come from Grace herself.

'I want to explore you,' she said.

He released her and, resting back on one elbow, stared down, wondering if this was another test Grace had decided she must put herself through. Closing his eyes, he traced the line of her full lips with his thumb pad as a reminder that Grace saw the world through touch now.

'Lie back,' she whispered.

This was the first time he had ever taken instruction in bed, but for Grace he would do pretty much anything right now.

She didn't just *learn* through touch he discovered, closing his eyes. Everything a sighted person could communicate with a glance Grace delivered with her hands. They were extraordinarily sensitive. They were such tiny hands, but so cool and strong. They had been as expressive as her eyes on the day they'd first met. He'd learned as much about himself as he'd learned about Grace in those few minutes.

'Stay still,' she told him.

Great though it was, this was a complete role reversal for him. No wonder it took some getting used to.

Having mapped his chest, she moved on to explore the

muscles of his arm and then his hands and fingers. It was
the most sensuous experience he'd ever had. When she
moved down the bed he held his breath as she stroked
his legs. He needn't have worried. She stopped her investigations a prudent distance up his thighs. But apart
from that she was a revelation. Some instinct seemed
to inform her where he felt the most pleasure and how
she must touch him to increase that pleasure. She could
tease and soothe in ways he had never imagined—ways
that sent his senses soaring to a point where it was he
who was in danger of losing control. Something that had
never happened in his life before.

'You're not supposed to do that,' he murmured, dragging her back into his arms.

'Not supposed to do what?' she said.

He kissed her, soothing her again. 'Grace?' he murmured seeing something was wrong.

'Did I do something wrong?' she asked in a small
voice.

He laughed softly against her mouth. 'You did nothing wrong. You did everything right—which is why we
need to pause.' There were tears in her eyes, he noticed.
'What haven't you told me, Grace?'

'It's the way you make me feel,' she said, biting her
lip. 'It frightens me.' Mashing her lips together, she gave
him that determined look of hers. 'And I'm crying because you kiss so damn well.'

He laughed. 'Then I'd better kiss you again,' he said.

When Nacho released her she realised how close she'd
come to telling him how she really felt about him—that
she wasn't even sure she could survive the strength of
her feelings for him. But she had to be realistic. After
devoting his life to his siblings, how could she burden
Nacho with a blind woman? It was selfish of her even to

think that way. She should save those wild emotions and channel them into something with a future attached—like her career.

She had promised everyone who had helped her that she would live her life to the full. Had that been just an empty pledge?

'Grace?' Nacho prompted, cupping her chin so he could stare into her face. 'What is it?'

'Nothing,' she lied, burrowing her face in his chest. 'I'm just trying to get something straight in my head.'

'And have you?'

Lifting her chin, she wished that she could see Nacho—so she could read him, so she could know him completely.

Feeling overwhelmed him when Grace reached for him. He was filled with a fierce determination to keep her safe and bring her pleasure.

Could those two things exist side by side?

'You taste of fruit,' she said, smiling as she kissed his shoulder. 'Kiss me,' she demanded fiercely, moving beneath him.

Grace's strength was what attracted him, he realised, that and her matchless femininity. Her face was radiant and her hair was tumbling around her shoulders in a billowing cloud. Moving it out of the way, he kissed her neck, before moving down the bed to rasp his stubble very lightly against the soft swell of her belly. Feeling her tremble, he kissed her again and she groaned, arching her hips as she searched for relief for the ache inside her. She tasted better than he remembered. She tasted of warmth and of woman and of Grace—unique and strong. Stripping her skirt off, he tossed it away. Her top followed. Now there was just a tiny lace thong between them. But he attended to her breasts first, suckling and relishing the taste of Grace and grape juice combined. When he lifted his head she allowed her thighs to part, as if she wanted him to see her arousal.

'How long must I wait?' she demanded, groaning in complaint.

'As long as I decide you must wait,' he said, enjoying the pleasure-pain as her fingers bit into his arms.

But she hadn't finished with him yet, and with an angry sound of frustration went straight for the button on his jeans. They were soon off, but he pinned her to the bed as she panted beneath him.

He had always thought sex should be fun, but this was the first time he had encountered a woman who could remotely match his appetite. 'Okay,' he said with amusement, somehow managing to keep her still. 'You win.'

'I don't want to win,' she said. 'At least not this game.'

This new Grace was free to be as provocative as she liked—free to express her feelings in a way she would never have dared to do before—and that made anything possible. The sensations she was experiencing in the darkness were dazzling.

Instead of moving she remained quite still. She wanted to remember every moment of this—Nacho's thigh brushing her just where she needed him, the intense little pleasure spasms engulfing her. He was a master of the art of seduction and she was a most willing pupil. Nacho knew exactly what he was doing, and was totally switched on to her needs as he prepared her for the ultimate pleasure.

'You're so cruel,' she complained on a shuddering breath as he talked to her in Spanish, no doubt promising all sorts of excess.

She exhaled with excitement, feeling the proof of his arousal rest heavy against her leg. He was massive. She

had always known he would be. But when she begged
him not to prolong the torture he only laughed.

'I'm being kind,' he assured her in a husky whisper.

He had never known a woman to be so full of desire.
When Grace rested in his arms, throwing her head back
as she was doing now to drag in air, he wanted nothing more than to pin her to the bed and pound into her
until they both fell back exhausted. But when she ran
those tiny hands across his chest, when she traced the
line of his shoulders with a touch so light, all he wanted
to do was to treat her exactly as she had asked him not
to—like cut glass. No woman had ever seduced him
with touch alone, but Grace could. She had magic in
her hands and something equally potent in her lovely,
lust-drenched face.

'Nacho?' she whispered, sensing the change in him.

The past had intruded without warning, and it had
come between them in the ugliest way. Throwing himself back on the pillows he wondered how he could even
think of doing this.

'Nacho, what's wrong?'

'What's wrong?' he said. 'You're not afraid of me,
are you, Grace?'

'Of course I'm not afraid of you. Why would I be?'

Because I destroy people, he thought. *Because I can
never give you what you want.*

Grace frowned with concern—*for him.* Since the tragedy he had always known it was his duty to devote his
life to family and to the vast territories they owned, and
that he must remain free of personal ties so that he could
never hurt anyone again.

'I think you've forgotten me,' Grace murmured.

He turned to look at her distractedly, and then she

touched him—not just with her hands, but with her indomitable will.

'Have you forgotten why you brought me here?' she
said, teasing him with a smile.

'Forgotten you?' The past fell away as he stared at
her. 'How could I ever forget you?' he murmured dryly.

'That's what I hoped you'd say,' she said, stroking him
in a way that made him forget everything.

'Tell me what you remember about me.'

'I remember you sluicing down in the yard,' she said.
'I remember your arms—so sexy, hard and muscular.'

'My arms are sexy?' he said, his lips pressing down
as he considered this information.

'Especially if they pin me down,' she said.

'Is that a hint?'

Grace's slender shoulders eased in a shrug. 'What
do you think?'

Kneeling between her legs, he eased the tiny lace
thong down over Grace's hips.

'What are you going to do?' she asked.

Surprised by the question, he was silenced for a moment—but then he realised Grace was in darkness, trusting him to keep her safe. 'I'm going to feast on you and
make you scream,' he said.

She laughed. 'See that you do,' she said.

His hunger was raging out of control, but he had only
teased her with the lightest of kisses when she cried out,
'Stop! I can't—'

'Hold on?' he supplied as she bucked beneath him.

'That's *your* fault,' she complained, still lost in pleasure as she gasped.

'I blame myself entirely,' he agreed dryly. 'More?'

'Of course,' she said.

Nacho was amazing. Shouldn't one tumultuous climax be enough for her? Shouldn't that have quietened the hunger inside her at least for a while? Instead it had grown, and with it her fantasies of what Nacho might do or make her feel next had exploded into endless possibility.

When she quietened he made some suggestions that turned her on beyond belief. 'Like this?' she said.

'Exactly like that,' Nacho confirmed when she drew her knees back.

'You like looking at me?' she guessed.

'I *love* looking at you,' he countered.

Feeling him move over her, she uttered a soft cry of excitement, and then he stroked her with just the tip of his erection, back and forth. Raising her arms above her head, she rested them on the bank of pillows. Reading her wishes, he took her wrists in one big hand while he guided himself inside her with the other.

'Oh, *please*,' she gasped.

'You're so small and I'm so big—'

'Yes,' she agreed, in a tone that suggested that was great news. 'More,' she encouraged as her excitement mounted.

'You're so pale, so soft, and your hands are so tiny.'

'And you're big in every way,' she said, remembering the weight of his erection as it flexed against her. 'And those big hands are the most delicate instruments of pleasure,' she added as he proved this to be true yet again. She groaned as each touch coloured in yet another frame in her imagination. 'And now it's my turn to explore you,' she insisted, freeing her hands to reach down— only to discover that, as she had suspected, Nacho was built perfectly to scale. One hand wasn't nearly enough to encompass his girth.

'Stop!' he ground out hoarsely.

Bracing her hands against his chest, she waited. And then cried out with shock as he moved. Had she thought she was ready for this? She could *never* be prepared for this, Grace realised, though Nacho was infinitely careful as he moved steadily deeper. When he inhabited her completely she gripped him fiercely with her muscles, triumphantly claiming him for her own.

'Good?' he murmured, brushing her lips with his.

'Can't speak,' she admitted on a shivering breath, wishing she could see the smile she knew would be curving his lips. But when he moved again she couldn't think, could only feel as she began to move instinctively in time with him.

'Don't hold back,' Nacho advised. 'Take as much time as you want. Take as much as you want.'

And with his promise in her head she fell with relief into mind-stripping release. Her fingers clawed at his back as she thanked him in words she had never used before.

'Again?' Nacho suggested with amusement, when she finally found some sort of holding area.

'Yes,' she breathed.

He made it no easier to hold on this time, and she fell the moment he entered her. He had made her greedy. He had made her want him more than ever. He had made her realise that her life from this moment on would be incomplete without Nacho in it.

'You *are* a witch,' he said when she used her muscles to keep him close.

Rocking into her, he drove the breath from her lungs in a muffled cry, and drove on until they both fell violently and gratefully into the darkness, tangled in each other's arms.

'Sleep?' Nacho suggested some time later, when she sucked in a shuddering breath.

A slow, sexy smile curved her lips. 'Not yet,' she whispered.

'Then ride me?' he suggested.

'All right. But don't help me.'

'I think we're a long way past that—don't you, Grace?'

Straddling him, she was turned on all over again by the way her legs were pressed wide by the size of Nacho's body. But being in control was the best. It felt great. Having his hands on her buttocks helping her to ride him to greater effect felt better still. She threw her head back, basking in sensation. Even now Nacho gave her little more to do than enjoy him. He understood exactly how to increase her pleasure with the subtlest encouragement from the pad of his forefinger as he rocked her back and forth. And thankfully he ignored her when she warned him that she couldn't hold out for long.

A wail of anticipation left her lips when she realised this was going to be fiercer and stronger than anything she had known so far. When she fell she must have blacked out for a moment, because she came round to find Nacho moving over her to an irresistible beat.

'Again,' he growled, and this time it wasn't a question.

He lost it right there. Sensation compacted into a nuclear force that shot from his core, engulfing him.

'Are you okay?' she said, when finally they were quiet again.

'I'm good,' he confirmed. 'You?'

He turned his head on the pillow to stare at Grace. The longing for her to see him had never been greater. He longed for her to know how she made him feel. He longed for her to see. But she couldn't see.

Cupping her face, he stroked her cheek and kissed her

mouth tenderly. 'You're a very special woman, Grace. Very special to me.'

'Unique, I hope,' she said, smiling in that way she had when she wanted to make light of things so they couldn't hurt her.

'You *are* unique,' he said fiercely, wanting her to feel his passion. Making love to Grace defied classification. There had to be some new word for it. Sex didn't even come close. 'I didn't hurt you, did I?' he said, his concern bringing tears in her eyes

'Only here,' she said, clutching her chest over her heart. 'Otherwise I'm fine.'

She said this wryly, with a small smile, and that smile tore at his heart, because he knew Grace would always say she was fine. She didn't want to be a trouble to anyone. She had probably reassured the doctors on the day they had told her she was going blind. But he guessed Grace bottled up her feelings and brought them out when she was alone to examine, and that thought stabbed him in the heart like a knife.

'How can you be fine if you're crying?' he said gruffly, blotting her tears with his thumb-pad.

'Because I'm not crying the way you think I am,' she said.

'And how is that?' he said as she turned her head on the pillow so they were facing each other. 'How many ways are there to cry?' As he spoke he traced the line of her jaw.

'You can cry from happiness,' she said. 'You can cry from feelings so big you can't express them in words. You can cry with amazement that anything can be so good.'

'Are you giving me a compliment?' he asked with amusement.

'Maybe,' she admitted wryly, still defensive, still frightened to commit herself entirely to anything that could bring her hurt. 'You're so gentle and caring…' Her face changed again. 'And so damn good in bed.'

He laughed as he dragged her close for more kisses.

'I didn't think I was capable of making love like that, or even feeling like that,' she admitted when he let her go.

'If there's one thing I've learned about you, Señorita Lundström,' he said, cupping Grace's chin and tilting her face so he could stare into her misty eyes, 'it's that you're capable of anything you set your mind to. Perhaps this isn't the right time to say it, but—'

'But you're going to say it anyway?' she guessed.

'Yes, I am. You've changed since we first met, Grace. You're stronger. You're more capable and more determined. Because you've had to be. I know that.'

'And because I was completely over-awed by you at the wedding—by everyone there,' she admitted. 'I felt so out of my depth. No wonder you thought I was naïve and awkward.'

'I thought you were beautiful.'

'Well, I felt like a fool. It was one thing being Lucia's friend, but being thrown into the type of society you Acostas inhabit—royalty, celebrities…'

'Who have exactly the same problems the rest of us do,' he pointed out.

'Not quite,' she argued wryly.

'So that accounts for your Cinderella flight?'

She laughed as she snuggled closer. 'I didn't feel safe with you then.'

'And now?'

She would never feel safe *without* Nacho again, Grace realised with concern. So much for standing on her own two feet. One night with Nacho and she was back to square one.

'What's wrong?' he said, feeling her tension.

She braced herself, and then told him the truth. 'I always think I've got this sight thing kicked, and then something happens and all the progress I've made counts for nothing.'

'Has that happened tonight, here with me?'

She shifted in his arms, knowing it was too soon to reveal her true feelings for Nacho, or how vulnerable she was. She'd just about convinced him she was strong. What would he think if he realised the truth? That where he was concerned she was utterly exposed, utterly defenceless?

'Hey,' he murmured in complaint when she turned away from him. 'Stop worrying about the future, Grace, enjoy *now*.'

He was right, she reasoned. 'Is that an order?' she said, turning back.

'Yes, it is.' He felt his heart squeeze tight as Grace reached out a hand to find his lips.

'You're smiling,' she said, tracing them.

It was one of those smiles Grace had talked about— the type of smile that could very easily have tears attached. 'I was just thinking we should get some sleep,' he said with no emotion in his voice. 'Tomorrow's a working day for both of us.'

'Liar,' she said. Her lips curved in a smile. 'You're thinking about making love again.'

Capturing her hand, he pressed a passionate kiss to her palm. 'You know me too well, Grace.'

'I wish,' she said quietly.

CHAPTER TEN

SHE woke in Nacho's big bed at the *hacienda* to find she was alone, and in those first waking moments she felt panic. It was like the early days, when she hadn't been able to get out of bed without falling over something— even in her own house. When she had first known she was losing her sight she had practised moving around the house wearing an eye mask, but she had always cheated. Peeping had become part of the routine. One day peeping hadn't been an option for her, and it wasn't an option now.

Nacho must be at the stables, she reasoned, trying to calm down. Lucia had said the stable yard was where her brothers lived, and that the houses they owned were for civilised people to inhabit. She felt for the nightstand, hoping there might be a phone there so she could maybe make an internal call, but there was nothing. And—

Oh, damn! Now she had succeeded in knocking her water over.

She wanted the bathroom, but didn't have a clue where it was, or how she'd make her way there.

She had to calm down. Sucking in some deep breaths, she concentrated on counting the Acosta residences. There was the *palazzo* on Fire Island, the penthouse in

London, and the main *estancia* Grace had visited for
Lucia's wedding—and here…

No good—heart still thundering.

Next she counted pianos. Four residences. Four pianos. There was a piano in every home because Nacho's
mother had used to play. Perhaps Grace could play one
of the pianos while she was here.

*Still hammering—hammering so hard now she could
hardly breathe.*

So now she thought through her favourite waltz, page
by page, bar by bar, note by note.

She really couldn't wait any longer. She would have to
find the bathroom—crawling if she had to. She'd done it
before. She knew that if she crawled around the perim-
eter of a room she would find doors and hopefully, eventually, the room she needed. Then a noise caught her ear.

'Buddy?'

Grace exclaimed with excitement. She had never been
so relieved to hear the scratch of claws on wood before. Nacho must have brought him up before he left so
she wouldn't be stranded. She'd been wrong to imagine Nacho would simply get out of bed and leave her to
it. She was right about him. He was caring. And sexy
as hell.

Feeling confident now, she turned her face into the
pillow to drag in Nacho's warm, clean scent. She smiled,
absorbing the contented ache of a body that had been
very well used. What a night! Nacho had revealed himself to Grace in ways she could never have imagined.
Who would guess there was such a tender, humorous
individual beneath that autocratic manner? Or that he
could be such an amazing lover…?

The hardest of the Acosta brothers?

She didn't think so. Nacho was wonderfully warm.

And she had relaxed properly for the first time in a long time, Grace realised as she stretched contentedly. She had learned a lot about herself too—like her insatiable capacity for passion. She felt womanly and appreciated, thanks to Nacho.

'Go find your harness, Bud,' she called, sitting up and swinging her legs over the side of the bed so she could test the floor with her feet. 'I bet he's brought it up...'

He had, and once she had Buddy to lead her around Grace moved swiftly to get ready for the day. She found her clothes neatly arranged on a leather sofa, and her toiletries waiting in the bathroom. Even her stick was propped against the sink, where she couldn't miss it.

'Someone has guessed that you don't go everywhere with me,' she told Buddy with amusement.

The shower had been left on an appropriate setting, and there was a stack of towels waiting for her on the side. She showered and dressed quickly, trusting her guardian angel had also matched up her clothes: jeans, sneakers, underwear and a tee, obviously brought over from the guest cottage. And then with Buddy's help she found her way down to a warm kitchen, fragrant with the smell of freshly baked bread. The room was alive with the chatter of at least two women.

Nacho's housekeepers, Grace presumed, greeting them brightly. 'Buenos días...'

'Buenos días, Señorita,' the women chorused gaily, ushering Grace into the room.

If the women wondered at Grace's sudden appearance in the main house they certainly didn't show it. Their welcome couldn't have been warmer. She heard the scrape of chair legs on a stone floor and felt Buddy's tug as he prepared to take her towards the seat that was being offered to her. Releasing him, she sat down.

The two women vied with each other to offer Grace every type of food and drink imaginable. Grace tried to find an appetite, so she didn't offend them, but all she could think about was when Nacho would be back. He would be out riding, she guessed, and one housekeeper, Maria, confirmed this. Señor Acosta was planning to meet Grace later that afternoon, Maria explained.

So long to wait! Grace hid her disappointment. She did have work to do, but first, if there was a piano in the house, maybe she could play it…

She asked the question and was surprised at the long pause. She wondered if it meant the two older women were exchanging glances. 'I understand if no one is allowed to play it,' she said, remembering the tragedy that had killed Nacho's parents, and the fact that Lucia had mentioned it had something to do with a piano. She couldn't imagine what—how could a piano and a flood be connected?—but Grace had never liked to probe around such a sensitive issue.

Maria had obviously come to a decision, as the housekeeper exclaimed, 'It would be *maravillosa*...wonderful to have music in the house again, *señorita*. The piano is in the hallway. Please, allow me to show it to you. But first I must find the key.'

Grace's excitement mounted. It had been so long since she had played a piano—since before she had lost her sight. So she wasn't even sure she still could. And she didn't really know why she had this sudden urge to play again, but she *felt* something here and knew she had to answer the longing. If she could only play for Nacho…

Her heart pounded with excitement at the thought as Buddy led her out of the kitchen and into the hall.

The hallway was big and fresh and filled with light. Grace always rejoiced that she still had a sense of light—

it made everything feel so much better. There was a flower display somewhere…she could smell the blossom. And beeswax. And floor polish. She smiled to think she would never have noticed things like that before. And that she would have found her rubber-soled sneakers annoying as they squeaked across the marble tiles, she realised, smiling wryly. She had so much to be grateful for.

Buddy brought her to a halt next to Maria, who was unlocking the piano. It was tucked beneath the grand staircase. No wonder she hadn't known it was there. Buddy had never had to make a detour round it. She felt for the piano stool, and then remembered that Nacho's mother would have been the last person to sit on it. It felt like a real privilege to be taking her place, hopefully playing the music that had once brought her and her children so much pleasure.

'I'm afraid the piano hasn't been played for years, *señorita*,' Maria murmured as Grace's hands hovered above the keys.

'That's what I thought,' Grace said quietly, thinking about the woman who had sat here before her. *I hope you don't mind me playing your piano*, she reflected silently. 'I haven't played for some time, either,' she explained to Nacho's housekeeper ruefully. 'I'm not even sure I *can* still play.'

Grace's heart squeezed tight when Maria touched her arm. 'I'm sure you can do anything you set your mind to, *señorita*.'

Grace could only hope Maria was right.

She sat for a long time without doing anything after Maria left. Putting off the moment, she guessed. The hall felt very quiet, very still, very empty. It was easy to imagine ghosts were listening. 'I don't want to let you down,' she murmured, reminding herself that all piano keys were set out in a logical sequence, so it should be no big deal that she couldn't see. The notes weren't going anywhere, and she could hear what she was playing just as well as she ever had. She just had to remember what Clark, the pianist at the club had told her. '*Close your eyes, Grace, and let the music flow...*'

What if it didn't flow?

It *would* flow, Grace told herself firmly. Nothing had changed since those nights at the club.

Everything had changed. Her fingers fumbled over the keys as if she was a toddler let loose on a piano. It didn't help that the instrument was so badly out of tune. She couldn't hear what she should be playing. She couldn't find her way into the tune—any tune. She couldn't trust her own judgement. Even the simplest nursery rhyme was beyond her reach.

This was ridiculous. She had to calm down and get over the fear. Dashing the tears away, she thought back to what they'd told her at the rehabilitation centre: she must always give herself time to think. Taking a deep breath, she tried again—first a scale, and then an arpeggio, and now a simple Chopin waltz, one of the slower ones she had always been able to play from memory. She started hesitantly, but her courage quickly grew. Clark Mayhew had been right. The music hadn't left her. It was still here in her head and in her fingers.

The hall was a natural amphitheatre, and even the suspect tuning seemed to add a poignant, haunting strain to the melody. The keys that had been sticking to begin with were working now, as if the piano was glad to be played again. Her heart began to soar as she played on. But then a door banged open and she jumped with alarm.

'Nacho?' She spun round on the stool.

Angry footsteps pounded across the hall towards her,

and she yelped with fright when Nacho slammed the piano lid down, narrowly missing her fingers.

'What are you doing?' she exclaimed, hugging herself defensively. His rage was buzzing around her like a swarm of angry bees.

'What am I *doing*?' he demanded hoarsely. 'Get away from the piano!' he roared as she ran her fingers along the edge of the lid with concern, feeling for damage. 'Get away from the piano, Grace.'

She was incapable of moving anywhere, and could only sit, stunned, wondering what had happened to her gentle lover from last night.

He couldn't believe Grace was still seated at the piano when he had insisted she must move away. His rational brain warned him that he was half mad with anger, grief, guilt, and that all of these were compounded by his concern for Grace, but the other part of him—the dark side that had once driven him to desert those he loved when he should have stayed to save them—said she must go. Just as Grace had made him forget the past last night, and the evil of which he was capable, she had brought it back to him today.

He would never have come back to the vineyards if it hadn't been to save his siblings' inheritance, and now he knew why. One by one he had forced himself to grow accustomed to all the familiar landmarks again, but the piano had always been at the root of the tragedy. And to hear it played again was torment beyond belief. He should have got rid of every piano in every house. Only the fact that if he had done so it would have created suspicion amongst his siblings had stopped him. He wouldn't do anything that might risk splitting his family when he had devoted his life to keeping that family together.

And Grace?

On the way to the house his head had been full of her. He hadn't been able to wait until this afternoon to see her. His only thought had been to be with her again. He had been aching to see her. But now he couldn't wait to send her away because he was frightened for her. He was frightened of the man he could be.

'I'm sorry,' she said with a helpless gesture. Grace's face was ashen. 'I'm not sure what I've done, Nacho.'

How could she be expected to know that when he'd walked into the house it was as if he had been thrown back in time to that fateful day when he'd heard his mother playing the piano? Or that what had happened next would shame him for ever? His brothers and sister would never forgive him if they knew what he'd done, and he was determined to keep their parents' memory intact. Lucia had been so young when they'd died. He wanted her to remember them like golden icons without fault or blemish, guardian angels watching over them.

'Nacho?'

Grace's voice was full of concern. *For him.* She was so unselfish. What did it matter if she was playing the piano?

'I didn't know you played,' he said distractedly.

'I didn't know I still could play,' she admitted.

Fresh guilt overwhelmed him when he heard her voice shaking and saw she was biting her lip. The tears in her eyes were proof enough that he must send her home, and quickly, before he destroyed her as he had destroyed his parents.

'Come away from the piano,' he said, as gently as he could.

'Of course,' she said, feeling for the edge of the seat. Every action she made now reminded him of how vulnerable she was, and how close he'd come to drawing Grace deeper into his dark world. He couldn't risk another tragedy.

'I'll ask Maria to help you collect your things so you can move back to the guest cottage,' he said. 'We have work to do this afternoon.' And thank goodness for it, he thought, longing for a return to something like normality.

'A tour of the vineyards?' she said, with some steel back in her voice.

'That's right,' he said, relieved that she seemed to have got over his shocking behaviour. 'And then, if you have all the information you need...'

'I can leave?' she said.

Her bewilderment stabbed him. 'Of course, if there's more research you have to do...'

'No,' she said, shaking her head. Drawing herself up, it was almost as if she drew a protective ring around herself. 'I'm sure I can complete my preliminary investigations this afternoon.'

But she couldn't sustain her composure and he found himself flinching when she seemed to fold in on herself.

'Can I ask you something, Nacho?' she said quietly.

'Of course.'

'What happened between last night and now?'

She didn't want to ask the question, but believed she deserved an answer, and when Nacho remained silent she drew the conclusion for herself. She could imagine him staring at her in bemusement. He was a man of the world who'd had sex with a woman. She was a woman who had made love with a man.

'What are you smiling about?' he said.

'I'm not smiling. I'm laughing at myself because I'm stupid.'

'You're not stupid, Grace.'

'Really?' she said. 'So I *didn't* read too much into last night, and imagine that we meant something to each other? Or is my piano playing just really bad?'

'This isn't funny, Grace.'

'You're telling me.' Her pain echoed round the hall. 'I think you owe me one thing,' she said. 'Can you tell me how you can be one person last night and another today? What have I done to make you so angry, Nacho?' She was all fired up and, turning to the piano, she made the lightest pass of her hand across the lid. 'I respect this instrument. I know it was your mother's, and I would never abuse her memory. I can't believe you think I would—'

'It's not that.'

'What, then? What have I done that's so terrible?'

Shaking her head, she let her anger burn out, and rested both her hands on the lid, bowing her head over them. He wished them both a million miles away. He wished he could be different. He wished Grace had never had to see him as he really was.

'I'm sorry,' she said, so softly he had to strain to hear her. 'I only wanted to find out if I could still play. You welcomed me into your home and I took advantage of your hospitality—no,' she said, stopping him with a raised hand when he tried to speak. 'I'm really sorry, Nacho. I didn't mean to remind you of such a difficult time in your life.'

A difficult time? It had been a murderous time, when he'd had murder in his heart.

'You weren't to know,' he said stiffly, cursing the day he had ever heard his mother play the piano.

Silence fell then, and a muscle flicked in his jaw as he stared at Grace. Her lips were still swollen from his kisses and her eyes were full of tears—tears *he* had put there. He had never wanted to comfort a woman more, but he knew that if he did that he would never let her go. *And he destroyed those he cared about.*

'Nacho?'

Grace's voice brought him back.

'Are you all right?' she asked him with concern.

She could still be concerned for him, he realised with incredulity. 'I'm fine,' he said brusquely, but his thoughts were in turmoil. He had been meaning to call Elias this very morning, to make some excuse so that Grace could stay. But now he knew he must send her away.

'At least speak to me,' she said.

'There's nothing more to say. You couldn't know about the piano,' he said stiffly. 'The lid should have been locked—'

'It was locked,' she said. 'I asked permission first, but please don't blame Maria.'

'It's no one's fault,' he managed somehow to grate out.

'Come on, Buddy.' Grace stood up.

'Wait—'

'No,' she said calmly. 'I'm here on business for Elias. So if you wouldn't mind…?'

He moved out of her way and the dog led her past. He watched Grace walk up the stairs with her head held high to collect her things. The irony occurred to him then. Unlike every other woman he had ever known, Grace really didn't need him.

As if to confirm this, she called back, without slowing her pace, 'Vineyards at two-thirty, Nacho.'

It was his turn to be on the back foot and wondering what last night had meant to Grace. 'I'll pick you up at two,' he said, calming the storm inside him.

'I'll make my own arrangements, thank you,' she called back.

* * *

She was confused by the piano incident, but wouldn't dwell on it. She knew from past experience that when she was as confused as this, as low as this, the only thing that would save her was launching herself straight back into life. It would be a life without Nacho in it, maybe, but she was going to do it by achieving one of her goals. Not a business goal, but a personal goal, and she would need Alejandro's help to do it.

What better time could there be to learn to ride independently, away from the safety of the corral, than when she was on her way to meet Nacho at the vineyard? Grace reflected, and she listened to Alejandro's instructions as he rode alongside her, with Buddy trotting at their heels.

To reassure both of them, Alejandro had explained, he was putting Grace's pony on a lead rein. 'So there are no unexpected hurdles for you to jump,' Alejandro had said, in the warm tone that always made her smile.

As if she hadn't jumped enough hurdles in Argentina already, Grace concluded, still feeling crushed and bruised after her encounter with Nacho. She had no answers for his behaviour, but now, with the breeze on her face like rare champagne, clean and clear with the fresh scent of blossom and lush green grass, she knew it was going to be a good day. She was determined it would be. The birds were singing, the frogs were croaking, and the wind played tag in the trees. What a great day, she told herself firmly. There was so much to enjoy. Why dwell on things she couldn't change?

If her heart would stop aching, maybe she could forget what had happened with Nacho.

'Nacho is also on horseback,' Alejandro explained, as if picking up her thoughts. 'That's why your pony's playing up. He can smell the stallion.'

Oh, good. Just when she thought she could forget

Nacho for five minutes he was back full force. 'Right,'
she said, nodding her head sagely, as if the information
Alejandro had just given her was useful rather than elec-
trifyingly, terrifyingly and painfully upsetting.

'I called ahead to explain that you would be riding to
meet him with me.'

Grace nodded her head, anxious now, although the
whole purpose of this afternoon was to visit the vines
with Nacho. But somehow, meeting him on horseback,
surprising him that she was riding alone outside of the
corral and without him behind her, felt a bit like wav-
ing a red rag to a bull. And she couldn't bear any more
confrontation. If they couldn't be lovers then at least let
them be friends—or, failing that, business associates
who were capable of being civil to each other.

'Are we close?' she said, feeling her pulse speed up.

'Grace.'

Very close, she realised.

'Hello,' she said, taking care to strip her voice of all
emotion.

'*Adiós, señorita!*'

'Are you leaving us, Alejandro?' Grace called out,
feeling a sudden moment of panic at being left alone in
her darkness with memory of Nacho's anger so fresh in
her mind. The sound of galloping hooves was her answer, though Alejandro called something back as he left.
'What did he say?' she asked, not even sure Nacho was
still there to answer her.

'Alejandro hopes that when you return to England
you will leave your heart in Argentina.'

There was no emotion in Nacho's voice as he said this,
and she couldn't see his expression to work out what he
was thinking. 'Who knows?' she said, feeling stung. 'If
the tour is successful today I might be back next year.

It would certainly be a pleasure to see Alejandro and Maria again.'

Another silence lengthened between them, and Grace found herself wishing for Nacho to break it. The horses were standing perfectly still for once, and she had lost track of where Nacho was in relation to her. There was nothing worse than this sense of being stranded somewhere she wasn't familiar with, and with a man who had shown such anger when she had done no more than play piano in his house.

'Nacho?' Her heart had begun to race with panic.

'I'm here,' he said. 'Let me help you to dismount.'

His voice was gentle, but though it reassured her, she wasn't ready to forgive him yet. She heard him spring to the ground close by, and now he was walking towards her, no doubt expecting her to wait until she could slide into his arms with relief. 'I know what to do,' she said. 'If you would just hold the pony steady for me?'

Her foot was *not* supposed to catch in the stirrup leather!

'Easy.' Nacho caught her before she hit the ground, but his only comment was, 'Swing your leg wider next time.'

So that was how it was going to be. She pulled herself together fast. 'Where are these new vines you want me to check?'

'This way,' he said.

'Which way?' she said, furious to feel her eyes welling up. 'I can't see where you're pointing.'

'So follow me,' he said. 'Here's Buddy's harness.' Freeing it from the saddle, where Alejandro had told her he had secured it, Nacho handed it to her. 'Would you like me to fasten it for you?'

'No, thank you. I can manage.'

'I dare say you can, but I don't have all day, Grace.'

She blinked, taken aback, but then realised she was so determined to do everything by herself it had never occurred to her that she might be holding other people up. 'I'll be as quick as I can,' she said, dipping down to secure the harness.

Forget heartache. Forget regret. Forget her feelings for the owner of this vineyard. They were irrelevant. She had always wanted to be accepted for who she was, with no allowances made for her being blind. Well, guess what? Nacho supported that wish of hers wholeheartedly. So, okay, now they understood each other. All that mattered now was making a successful survey of the Acosta vines for Elias. All that mattered now was business.

CHAPTER ELEVEN

GRACE was about ten minutes into the tour when she found a problem with the vines.

'What do you mean, you're not happy with the vines?' he demanded when she continued to frown.

'I mean you've got a problem,' she said.

'Well, I can't see anything wrong,' he argued impatiently as he scanned the lush wall of green vines.

'Neither can I,' Grace reminded him with an edge.

'So what *is* the problem?' he said, frowning as he imagined some small alteration to the hydration system, possibly. He exclaimed when she yanked off a yard of vine.

'*This* is your problem,' she said. 'You'll have to destroy this area and isolate it, then spray the rest of your vines with an organic pest control.'

'What the hell are you talking about? They look fine to me. A little dry, perhaps—'

'A *little* dry?' she said, crumbling one of the leaves in her fist and tossing the dust into the air. 'If I'm right, this leaf is providing bed and board for a bug. But as I can't see it I'll need you to confirm my suspicions. Well?' Unfurling another withered leaf, she held it out on her palm.

He cursed beneath his breath when he saw the tiny

bug nesting inside. 'You're right,' he confirmed. 'How could this have happened without anyone noticing?'

Grace's slender shoulders lifted in a shrug. 'This sort of infestation is practically impossible to detect in a forest of green until it takes hold—by which time it's usually too late to do anything about it. But if you run your hands over the vine you can feel the rogue leaves quite easily. I'm guessing your people have been checking them with a ride-by, or on foot?'

His jaw clenched as he accepted she was right.

'Well?' she said. '*Is* that what they do?'

He had to shake himself. He had been staring into Grace's upturned face, thinking she would be gone soon and safe from him, but now he was thinking, *Dios! She'll have to stay and see this thing through.* Torture for him, danger for her.

'Nacho?' she prompted.

'Yes, that's what they do,' he confirmed. 'I realise we'll have to change our procedures. It seems I owe you an apology, Grace.'

'It seems you do,' she agreed.

Touch had served her well again. If they had found this infestation in time, Grace had potentially just saved the vineyard. As the silence lengthened between them his gaze slipped to her lips. He could still taste her on his mouth and remember how she had felt beneath his hands—

'I'll make a call,' she said, crunching another leaf to powder in her hand.

Grace called a scientist who was an expert in viticulture the moment they got back to the house.

'She'll be here tomorrow,' Grace confirmed, ending the call.

'Then what?'

'If I'm correct, she will prescribe the correct spray to use, and then we wait.'

'For how long?'

Grace hesitated. 'A month or so.'

'Will you stay on?'

'I think I have to, don't you?' she said, in the same business-like tone. 'The result of the final survey will be crucial to both sides. Don't worry, I'll book into a hotel. Did I say something funny?' she demanded when he began to laugh.

'Only that the nearest hotel is around three hundred miles away. You'll have to stay here, Grace.'

She said nothing to this, and he felt bad laughing when Grace couldn't know the extent of the land they were standing on. She couldn't see that it stretched to the horizon, where it was bound by the snow-capped Andes, or that it extended for hundreds of miles on either side.

'You can stay on at the guest cottage.'

'Not if I'm in your way.'

'You won't be in my way, Grace.'

No, because Nacho would steer clear from now on, she imagined.

'That's settled, then,' she said, acting as if her heart hadn't been trampled on and business was all that mattered.

The expert arrived the next morning, as Grace had promised, flying in on Nacho's jet to the Acostas' private landing strip. He shook the woman's hand with relief and they strolled through the rows of vines deep in conversation.

'This is in no way finished yet,' the expert informed him. 'Grace has been correct in every detail, but we won't know for some time if the spray I have prescribed is effective. I suggest you keep Grace here and I'll come back in about a month—unless Grace needs me to return sooner.'

The irony of Grace suddenly being in charge didn't escape him. The thought of her staying on was both a relief and a concern, because he still wanted her desperately—even though he believed he was an inherent risk to her.

'At least the damage to the vines isn't irreparable,' Grace pointed out.

'And nowhere as bad as I feared,' he agreed, wondering if those dark circles beneath Grace's eyes meant she had tossed and turned all night like him.

'But you were right to call me,' the forensic viticulturist assured him, distracting him as she came to shake him by the hand again before leaving. 'It could have been a lot worse without Grace's prompt action, but if you remove those rogue vines and spray, the rest the problem should be eradicated.'

'And we should know this in around a month?' he confirmed, glancing at Grace, who showed no emotion.

'That's correct,' the scientist told him. 'Well…your jet's waiting to take me back,' she said, 'so I'll leave you two to organise the spraying and see you both again in a month.'

This was turning out to be the longest month of her life. Concern for the vineyards competed with the ache in her heart, resulting in a constant nagging pain. If it hadn't been for horse riding, and the kindness of Alejandro and Maria, she would have gone stark, staring mad, Grace concluded.

Nacho avoided her for much of the time, though every morning when she got up to check the vines to be sure the spray was doing its job she would invariably find he

was already there before her. He had organised teams of
workers to examine each plant, and she wouldn't have
been surprised to discover that he came here each night
to bathe each individual leaf in spray. The vineyard
meant so much to him.

This morning was no different from the rest, she re-
alised, patting his grazing horse as she walked past.
'Nacho?' she said, feeling her way along the row of vines.
She'd left Buddy with Nacho's horse to keep it company.
She found she moved faster on her own now she knew
every inch of the vineyards intimately.

'I *won't* let my people down,' Nacho exclaimed
fiercely, without pause for *hello, good morning* or *how
are you today?* 'This might have started as a project to
ensure the financial future of my brothers and sister and
their families, but these people...'

When Nacho paused, Grace guessed he was making
a gesture that encompassed all of the land and the cot-
tages on it.

'They mean everything to me, Grace,' he went on, the
passion mounting in his voice with every word. 'They
are fighting alongside us to keep this place running and
we can't let them down, you and I.'

The thought that they were fighting side by side made
her more determined than ever to see this through. She
could sense his desperation to preserve the livelihoods
of his staff, and for a brief moment they stood together—
one mind, one determination, one goal.

'What do you think of the progress so far?' he said.

She ran her hands over the nearest vine. The signs
were good, but she had to tell him honestly, 'It's too
soon to be sure yet.'

'You won't tell Elias?'

'I haven't yet.' Though putting off the moment was

getting harder as Elias grew ever more impatient for her report. 'I'll check the rest,' she said, moving past him as she reminded herself that checking the vines was what she was here for this morning.

'I won't get in your way,' he said.

And so another day without Nacho in her life passed, followed by another long, lonely night. A whole month of waiting anxiously, watching the vines and keeping their distance from each other with plenty of longing, yearning and worrying as they gave the spray time to work, interspersed with bouts of frustration and bewilderment on Grace's part at the change in Nacho. This last concern usually culminated in jaw-grinding anger. She wasn't a saint, and she didn't have a clue what she'd done wrong. Was playing the piano such a sin? Nacho had given her no inkling as to why he had changed so completely towards her between one day and the next. The end result? More sleepless nights, more anxious days.

And now, quite suddenly, or so it seemed, the expert was due back tomorrow.

They stood together as the scientist left, waiting until Alejandro had driven the Jeep away to the airstrip before either of them showed any emotion.

Nacho was the first to speak. '*Dios*, Grace, I can't believe it.'

'A clean bill of health,' Grace murmured, feeling her legs might give way with relief as she sent up fervent thanks.

Inside she was rejoicing, whilst still feeling the exhausting effects of a month of tension—not all of it brought about by waiting for the spray to work. A month of keeping her distance from Nacho hadn't lessened her feelings for him, but they couldn't go on like this. She'd be leaving soon, but if everything went well Elias would insist she made regular visits. She had to make her peace with Nacho even if she still wasn't sure what she'd done wrong. Whatever it was, she couldn't balk at this last hurdle.

'Truce?' she said, extending her hand in his general direction.

'Truce,' Nacho agreed, clasping it.

He seemed reluctant to let her go, and she couldn't bring herself to let him go. Moments passed—it could only have been a split second in reality—before they broke apart.

'So we're free for what's left of the day,' she said, feeling awkward suddenly. They hadn't had any spare time on their hands for a month. Every day since she had discovered that bug in the leaf had been ruled by hourly walk-pasts, checking, testing, spraying again, and waiting. Now they could relax and turn the maintenance programme over to Nacho's staff.

'I'm hungry,' he said.

She heard the frown in his voice and realised that this return to normality wasn't easy for either of them. 'We do need to eat,' she confirmed, thinking of the snatched meals both of them had taken in the kitchen whenever they got a chance.

'And I should say thank you to you,' Nacho remarked.

'Well, thank goodness you've got something to thank me for,' Grace said, smiling. She sensed they were both smiling for the first time in a month.

'Alejandro rode here with you?' he said as they walked back towards the horses.

'Yes, and then he went back for the Jeep. Could you hold Buddy's harness while I mount up?'

'Why don't I buckle Buddy's harness onto my saddle and then help you mount up?' Nacho suggested.

She smiled again—ruefully this time. 'I thought you'd know better than to ask by now.'

'And I thought you'd know better than to refuse,' he said.

She was still smiling when he helped her into the saddle.

'So where are you planning to take me?' she said, gathering up the reins.

'To eat.'

'That's not very helpful. Do I need to change?'

'You're fine as you are,' he said, thinking that Grace was more than fine, she was beautiful—a fact he had fought to ignore for the past month and lost. 'This is the first time I've taken you out,' he said, springing into the saddle.

And she could get *that* rogue thought out of her head right away, Grace informed her inner voice firmly. This was nothing like a first date.

Unfortunately, her heart refused to agree with this premise, and insisted on thundering painfully in her chest. She tried persuasive tactics: lunch would be a really great opportunity to cement their fledgling business relationship.

Oh, really?

Her heart went wild as her pony fell in step with Nacho's stallion. The relief and sheer exhilaration they both felt now the vineyard had been saved made this feel exactly like a first date.

'Is it far?' she said, hoping there would be a chance for her to calm down before they arrived.

'Not far at all. I hope you're not going to be disappointed. It's not much of a place for celebration. It's just a little *cantina* up in the hills, with a lot of local atmosphere attached.'

'Just as long as the food is good,' she said, suddenly realising how hungry she was. Had she even sat down long enough to eat a proper meal in a month?

'The food is excellent and the wine is even better.'

'From the Acosta vineyards?' she guessed.

Nacho confirmed this. 'And there's music, should you feel like dancing.'

As he spoke, Grace's dog positioned itself between them like some self-appointed chaperon.

'Okay, Buddy. Safety's always at the forefront of my mind, too.' He started to clip the lead rein on to the pony's bridle.

'If that's the rope,' Grace said, hearing the click of the catch, 'I don't need it.'

'Grace—'

'Alejandro says so,' she insisted, batting his hand away. What do you think I've been doing for the past month? I've ridden to the vineyards every day. I have to do this on my own. Alejandro trusts me. Don't you?'

Leaning over, he removed the rope. 'No cantering and no surprises, Grace.'

'I certainly hope not,' she agreed.

As Grace turned to say this and her gaze missed his face he remembered again everything she was, and everything he had been missing this past month while they'd been working. One thing was for sure: Grace never allowed anything to hold her back. He'd missed their verbal jousting.

'Hey, hold up,' he warned when Grace took off. 'If you trot as fast as that he'll bounce you right off.'

'And if you won't let me canter what else am I supposed to do? I'll be a mile behind you at this rate.'

He looked at the fixed set of Grace's mouth and re-alised it probably matched his own. 'Infuriating woman,' he muttered, bringing both horses to a halt. 'What part of *no* don't you understand?'

'Am I going too fast for you, Nacho?' Grace said with a defiant smile, lifting her chin.

'I think I can keep up,' he murmured. The look he gave her had stopped grown men dead in their tracks—but then he remembered. Nothing about Grace made it easy to remember she couldn't field those looks and bounce them straight back at him.

'Well?' she pressed. 'Are you ready to canter yet, Nacho?'

He barked a laugh. 'You're not good enough to take the lead yet.'

'But soon,' she said, laughing as she tossed the hair out of her eyes.

He saw no reason to doubt her.

CHAPTER TWELVE

'ARE you still there?' Grace mocked him.

'I'm still here,' he confirmed, noting how well she was managing the horse. Just seeing her in the saddle was enough to fire his blood. So much for not allowing Grace to get too close. He had always said half stubbornness and half instinct made a good rider, and Grace had both. 'You're making good progress,' he granted. If he gave her any more encouragement, knowing Grace, she'd bolt for the hills. 'Loosen the reins and make your hands softer. That's better.'

She blushed at his praise—which took his mind back to the last time he'd seen her face flushed, and led on seamlessly to how it had felt to have Grace's hands on his body. Thinking about that was enough to shake his resolve about sending her home now the vines had a clean bill of health.

'I told you it would be all right,' she called back to him. 'You have to start trusting me, Nacho.'

'And you have to learn to walk before you can canter.'

'Gallop, don't you mean?' she said, urging her pony on.

'Enthusiasm is great, but I'm still going to curb you.'

'I wish you luck with that,' she said, flinging the challenge at him as she rode even faster.

And risk her safety? *Never,* he determined as he urged his stallion to chase Grace's pony down.

'Spoilsport,' she said as he drew level.

'I'm saving you from yourself, Grace,' he said, taking charge of her reins.

She was excited and breathing heavily, and she stirred his blood like no one else. But he'd lived with his barriers too long to break them down now, despite how much he wanted her. 'Do as I say,' he warned, 'or this riding lesson is over. Do I make myself clear?'

'Perfectly,' she said, in a voice still full of defiance.

Was she supposed to like Nacho's stern tone quite so much? Grace wondered. She *liked* standing up to him. She *liked* having a wall to kick against and had missed it during their long month of separation. She settled for riding sensibly, knowing Nacho was probably right. They were both high on victory after the expert's verdict on the vines and feeling invincible right now.

She heard the *cantina* long before they arrived. She could hear the clop of shoes on a raised wooden floor and plates clashing above the racket of good-natured chatter. And just as Nacho had said, there was music—rustic and catchy. A local group, she guessed.

'Okay for you, Grace?' Nacho said, seeing her interest as he sprang down.

'The sounds take me back to the days when I was a waitress,' she admitted.

'Happy days?' he asked, taking her pony's reins over its head.

'Very,' she said, thinking about it. 'I miss the people—and don't forget I met Lucia while I was working as a cocktail waitress. Are you sure I don't look too scruffy?'

'You look great,' he said, helping her to dismount. 'I'll

take the horses and we'll leave Buddy here in the shade. I'll have some water and a steak sent out.'

She laughed. 'Are you trying to get round my best friend?'

'Could be...'

While they waited for their food they talked business—not as bad as it sounded, as they were two equals talking now. Grace had earned Nacho's respect, and their shared interest in saving the vineyard gave them plenty to talk about. And then they didn't talk business. They laughed—something neither of them had done for ages. Laughter shared was closeness too, Grace thought as they relaxed into each other's company. It had been far too long since they'd had a chance to relax.

And then the elderly owner of the *cantina* took Grace by surprise by suggesting that she dance with Nacho, forcing her to make up a couple of golden rules on the hoof: laughter? Yes. Dancing? No. She would never be ready for that. Dancing with Nacho? Being close to him again?

'I'm not sure that's wise,' she said diplomatically. 'I've got two left feet.'

'Fortunately I've got one of each,' Nacho murmured, drawing Grace away from the table.

And now she was on the dance floor, with Nacho's arms around her, remembering...remembering everything, Grace realised as she tried to catch her breath. The only certainty was that his remembered touch was nothing like the real thing. This was so much better, and she was instantly responsive to Nacho's sensitive hands.

To the music, Grace told herself firmly.

'Relax, Grace.'

How could she relax when she was remembering the morning after they'd made love, when Nacho had grown so cold and remote? How could she relax when she didn't have to see the effect Nacho had on other women to know he would be the centre of attention now? How could she relax when she felt like *this* about him?

'You dance well, Grace.'

How could anyone not dance well in Nacho's arms? Even locked in darkness she could feel the rhythm flowing through them. She moved instinctively with him, gaining courage with every step, though it was nothing short of a miracle that she could concentrate at all now she had discovered Nacho was wearing a tight-fitting shirt that left very little to the imagination of her all-seeing hands. It was a struggle to keep a clear head, and a struggle to know what to think when Nacho remained tantalisingly elusive. When she wanted him to drag her close he held her at a safe distance, and when she contrived to let the music bring them together naturally, his touch remained frustratingly impersonal. But, however clever Nacho might be at keeping them just that little bit apart, even he had no answer for the electricity between them—and that was as real and as exciting as it had ever been.

It was only when the music ended and they returned to the table that she realised they had developed a sort of shorthand between them. Nacho touched her arm and she knew when they were approaching her chair. Another touch and she knew roughly where that chair was, could feel for it and sit down. He had a sixth sense for when she wanted help and when it wasn't welcome.

When his shadow crossed her depleted vision she thanked him for the dance, though she guessed they both knew it had been a lot more than that. This time in the *cantina* had allowed them to rebalance their relationship, giving them chance to start over. *Maybe...*

'I really enjoyed that,' she admitted.

She felt the shift of air between them as he bowed ever so slightly in return. 'My pleasure, *señorita*,' he said coolly.

They were so close, so in tune, and yet something vital was missing. There was a chasm between them only the past could fill, and it would take some serious explaining on Nacho's part to do that, Grace realised as their food arrived and the past was something she couldn't force him to talk about.

Navigating a meal was always fraught with potential disaster. And now it turned out she had chosen the messiest food on the menu and was paying the price for it, Grace realised as Nacho rubbed one firm thumb-pad across the swell of her bottom lip.

'Crumbly *empanadas*,' he explained dryly when she drew a fast breath in.

So, not the irresistible attraction of her bee-stung lips?

After the release of tension at the vineyards and the fun they'd had since, chatting and dancing at the cantina, finishing the meal seemed to bring with it a new sort of tension. They had reached the *where-do-we-go-from-here*? point, Grace thought, feeling ready to scream by the time they walked outside. If Nacho wanted to start planning her homeward journey, he only had to say.

'About my flight home—' she said.

What happened next wasn't so much a conscious decision on his part as a reflex action, Nacho realised as he swept Grace off the ground and settled her on the saddle in front of him.

'You could have warned me,' she said, panting with shock as she laughed.

'Why?'

Grace only shook her head and smiled at his arrogance. 'What about my pony?' she said.

'They'll stable him here overnight. Don't worry, Grace, everything is taken care of.'

'Including me?' When he said nothing to this, she added, 'Should I be alarmed, Nacho?'

'Possibly,' he said, tightening his arm around her waist.

'And what about Buddy?' she exclaimed.

'He's coming with us.'

'Coming with us *where*?' she pressed. 'Look, you only have to say. I can pack and be ready to leave as soon as your jet is ready to take me—'

'I don't want to talk about your travel plans, Grace.' This couldn't go on any longer, he realized. Not when they'd been through so much together. 'I need to tell you why I want you to go home.'

'*Why* you want me to go,' she said.

The pain in Grace's voice shamed him after all she'd done for the Acostas, but he couldn't risk taking her into the dark place he inhabited. Just hearing that self-doubt creeping back into Grace's voice was proof of how easily he could wipe out everything she had achieved since her illness. He wanted to reassure her that she had done nothing wrong, that the fault lay with him. Whatever he might feel for Grace, the past would always stand between them. But if he didn't tell her the truth now he would destroy her too.

He rode past the guest cottage and on to the riverbank that held so many memories for him. It was the best place—in fact, the only place—to tell her what he must.

But as he dismounted and turned back to help her down, Grace launched herself from his horse. Almost falling as she reached the ground, she stumbled away from him.

'Grace—wait.'

Her dog, bewildered and uncertain for once, came to sit by his heels and looked up at him. 'Come on, Buddy,' he exclaimed, starting to run. Did she even know where she was going? Grace had left the path and was clambering down the embankment towards the river. Fear raged through him as she grew closer. 'Grace, stop! Come back!'

Memories tumbled on top of one another like an avalanche of guilt, burying him alive as he raced through brambles and over branches to get to her before it was too late. Grabbing her with relief, he hugged her to him as if he would never let her go.

'I'm all right,' she insisted angrily, her voice muffled against his chest.

'You almost fell into the river!'

'I didn't,' she said, still trying to push him away.

'You mustn't run off like that, Grace—'

'What's it to *you*?' she demanded.

'I care about you,' he said, releasing her.

'Then don't,' she said, appearing to attack her clothes rather than straighten them. 'How do you think I manage when you're not around?'

'Please just try and be sensible for once.'

'*Sensible*?' she exclaimed. 'Was I was sensible when I went to bed with you?'

He felt his heart wrench as her blank eyes searched his face. 'Grace—'

'Don't,' she said, shaking her head and turning away.

To hell with that. Catching hold of her wrists, he dragged her back again. 'I don't regret one single moment of making love to you, and I hope you don't regret it either. Well?' he ground out fiercely. '*Do* you regret it, Grace?'

'No,' she raged with matching fire, 'not for one second. But I don't understand how you blow hot and cold. You've barely spoken to me for a month, Nacho. We've achieved something incredible together at the vineyards, and we've had fun celebrating our victory at the *cantina,* and now, just when I think everything is back to normal between us, the curtain comes down.'

He had no answer for her. Well, he did, but it involved telling her about another time by the river that hadn't ended so happily.

Grace had gone still, and he stiffened as she folded like a leaf. Sinking to her knees on the damp earth, she whispered, 'I'm sorry, Nacho. This isn't about me. Please forgive me. I've grown selfish since I've lost my sight.'

With a roar of denial he swept her into his arms. Cupping her chin, he stared into her eyes even though he knew she couldn't see him. 'Selfish is the very last thing I'd call you, Grace. You worked to help save the vineyard and ensure its recovery along with everyone else. You were out every morning at dawn and you didn't stop working until the sun went down. You've been there for us every step of the way. You're the one who should be celebrating, Grace—for what you've achieved. We should all be celebrating.'

'So why aren't you?' she said.

He took a long pause. 'I have something to tell you first,' he said.

'About your past?'

He grimaced. 'I hate things that can't be changed,' he murmured, thinking back.

'You mean you hate things *you* can't change,' Grace argued gently.

He gave a faint smile of acknowledgement—one she couldn't see—and as the seconds ticked it gave him a chance to realise that even his past seemed insignificant when compared with what Grace had had to face.

'And you?' he said. 'What about you, Grace? Nobody ever gets round to asking about you.'

'You're changing the subject,' she said wryly.

'I know,' he whispered, drawing her back into his arms.

She resisted him briefly and weakly, and then she sighed and relaxed. 'So what do you want to know?' she said, resting her head on his shoulder.

'Let's start with everything,' he said.

She laughed as he drew her down onto the bank at his side. 'There's not much to say. I was an only child, a dreamer with a lot of time on my hands. I spent most of that time reading and playing the piano.'

'And your parents?'

'My parents were wonderful—my mother still is. I had a wonderful childhood, but then my father died and my mother remarried—happily, I'm pleased to say.' She shrugged. 'That's about it, I'm afraid.'

That was far from *it*, he thought. He left it a while and then asked, 'Did your father's death upset you greatly?'

'Of course.' She went quiet and then added, 'I felt terrible when we lost Dad, and guilty that I wasn't there for him when he died. I was playing at a concert,' she explained ruefully. 'It all seems so pointless now—'

'Not pointless, Grace. I'm sure your father would have been very proud of you.'

She pressed her lips together, half-smile, half-grimace. 'My mother met someone else quite quickly. He had his own family and they moved into our old house. My bedroom became someone else's bedroom while I was away—don't,' she said, sensing his concern on her behalf. 'It was time for me to move out—too late for me to become part of a new unit.'

'But surely when you became ill—?'

'Are you suggesting everyone should have dropped their own life and rallied round? Why would I expect them to?'

Because they're your family, he thought, knowing that was exactly what his family would do, realising how lucky they were to have such a tight family unit.

'By the time I became ill my mother was on a dozen committees—my stepfather was on even more. Why would I ask them to step in and sort out my life? No one could learn the things I had to learn except me. So what if I had a few more hurdles to jump than I anticipated?'

'Grace—' he scolded.

'I've got wonderful friends like Lucia,' she said, refusing to be kept down. 'I've got my health and a job I love—as well as the best guide dog in the world. I've got a fantastic life, Nacho. I wouldn't change a thing.'

'And you've still got your music,' he pointed out.

Grace went quiet. They both did. He had given her the cue she had been waiting for. 'Why did me playing the piano upset you so much?' she asked him bluntly. 'Were you reminded of your mother?'

'I never speak about my personal life,' he said, backing off from his earlier decision.

'Too late,' she said as she heard him brush grass and debris from his riding breeches. 'You promised to tell me why I must go. You can't go back on that now. You owe me that much.'

'I owe you a lot more,' he said.

'So tell me what you have done that's so terrible,' she said, confident she would find the right words to destroy

Nacho's demons. Goodness knew she had fought off enough of her own. 'Nothing you can say can shock me.'

'I killed my parents,' he said.

CHAPTER THIRTEEN

IT WAS one of those moments when Grace realised she had no answers, no help to give. She felt as much at sea as she had when the doctor had told her she was going to go blind. A total inability to arrange her thoughts into any sort of useful order left everything a jumble in her mind. Feelings? She had those—and to spare. But when it came to practical answers she had none.

They sat in silence for a long time, and when the fog began to clear she asked the only question she could. 'Can you tell me what happened?'

Nacho took so long to answer she wondered at first if he hadn't heard her, but then he said, 'My late father's life has been well documented in the gutter press, so I guess you already know he wasn't a god.'

'And your mother?' she said carefully, sensing this was where the trouble lay—or why would the piano figure so prominently in Nacho's mind?

'She was left alone while my father was away playing polo.'

'And she was lonely?' Grace guessed, trying to imagine what it must have been like to be a young woman with small children in a foreign country, far away from those she loved. Isolating, but not insurmountable, she thought, remembering the friendliness she had encountered in Argentina. But it wasn't for her to read the past, or judge a woman she didn't know. 'We're not so different, you and I.'

'Meaning?'

'Meaning we both keep a lot hidden inside.'

'Everyone has secrets, Grace, but not everyone has your mountains to climb.'

'Don't worry about me,' she said and then she laughed. 'I've got a great set of crampons.'

She reached for his hand and almost missed it. He took her hand in both of his and linked their fingers. 'Turns out my mother wasn't the flawless icon I believed her to be.'

'You mean she was human?' Grace suggested wryly.

'More than,' he agreed, feeling a surge of contentment as she snuggled close to him. 'But I was naïve.'

'It was a long time ago,' Grace pointed out, pulling away and turning her head, as if she could look at him and receive confirmation of this. 'Are you mistaking young and idealistic for naivety?' she said. 'Tell me.'

'There's not much more to say.'

'Oh,' she said. 'So telling me that you killed your parents is not much…?'

She didn't press the point. She didn't need to. She turned her face to the river, where she heard some birds play-fighting—or maybe it was a mating dance. They were certainly making a lot of noise as they flew back and forth, scraping their wing-tips across the surface of the river as they dipped and soared. It was a special moment. It would be one of those rare events that wildlife photographers waited days to film.

And Grace couldn't see it.

'Tell me the rest, Nacho,' she said.

Turning his mind from Grace's constant battles he

thought back to the past, to the last time he'd heard his mother play the piano. 'On the day of the tragedy I was riding past the *hacienda* while my mother was having her music lesson. I couldn't wait to get off my horse and tell her how much I admired her musicianship. By the time I barged into the house she was in bed with her music teacher—a vain man, who made no secret of his contempt for the wild Acosta children.'

He paused, and even huffed a laugh as he remembered the next bit. It was hard to imagine he had been such a fool.

'Hearing my mother's cries, I burst into her bedroom to rescue her—only to realise they were cries of pleasure.' Grace wasn't smiling, he noticed. He was glad of that. He shrugged. 'That's it.'

'That isn't it,' Grace argued. 'That's no way *it,* Nacho.'

'There are no words—' There truly weren't.

She waited in silence.

'I didn't know my father was on his way home, or that he almost killed the music teacher when he found him with my mother before throwing him out. My mother screamed at my father and told him that she was leaving him for the music teacher and she left the house with him in a blaze of anger. None of us knew the river had burst its banks…'

'And then the flood came?' Grace prompted.

He gave a shuddering sigh as he thought back. 'They would have got away—but my mother insisted on going back into the house to get a ring my father had bought her. Maria told me that. When news reached us that she and her lover had been swept into the water the staff tried to launch a rescue. My father rushed out to try and save her, but the flood water was too fast and too deep. It swept all three of them to their deaths.'

'And where were you?' she said.

'Galloping as far and as fast as I could away from the house, with the devil on my back.'

'But you knew none of this until later,' Grace pointed out. 'You didn't kill your parents, Nacho, and you mustn't think that. The flood killed your parents. Nature killed your parents.'

'I could have saved them if I'd been here,' he insisted.

'Nacho,' she said, sitting back, 'you just have to accept there are some things you can't control.'

He was silent for a long time, and then he said, 'Like you, Grace?'

As the tension slowly eased between them she relaxed.

'You should stay,' he said. 'Stay on here, Grace. Help me to build the vineyards into something we can both be proud of.'

Hugging her knees, she smiled ruefully and shook her head.

'I'm asking you to stay,' he said. Taking both her hands in his, he broke the habit of a lifetime to plead for what he knew was right. 'I'm asking you to stay in Argentina with me. You don't have to go back to England. I'll take care of you.'

'No!' she exclaimed, pulling her hands free. 'Just listen to yourself, Nacho. I don't want anyone to *take care of me*. I'm not an invalid.'

'I phrased that badly.'

'No,' she said again—more fiercely than before. 'You phrased that exactly as you meant it to sound.'

'What's wrong with wanting to protect you and care for you?' he demanded. 'Do feelings frighten you, Grace?'

'No. *This* frightens me,' she said, sweeping a hand

across her eyes. 'Were you ever frightened of the dark, Nacho?'

He shook his head, feeling more ashamed at his ignorance of how Grace must be feeling than he had after his own tragedy.

'And if you lived in permanent darkness like me?' she said.

'I couldn't begin to imagine it,' he admitted.

'I used to think I'd know what it was like to be blind—back in the days when cheating was still possible and I put an eye mask on to perform a few simple tasks around the house. Have you ever tried balancing things on a tray with your eyes shut?'

'Grace—all I'm trying to say is that you don't have to be alone.'

'But I *am*,' she said, sounding distraught as she covered her face with her hands. 'I'm alone in *here*,' she insisted, shaking her head.

'What do you miss most?' he said fiercely, determined to shake her out of this. 'Come on, Grace—tell me!' Forced to resort to plucking her fingers from her face, he held them firmly in his as he demanded again, 'What do you miss the most, Grace?' He wanted her to taste the same freedom he did after dealing with the past—that sense of being like a helium balloon, flying high and free. 'Grace?' he prompted. 'Tell me.'

'Clouds,' she said suddenly.

He held his breath, certain she would come back to him.

'That's what I miss the most,' she said. 'I miss staring into the sky and deciding what the shapes are—I miss watching them scudding by to who knows where? I bet your mother used to look up and wonder if those same clouds were going to travel to where your father was. She must have been so lonely and frightened, Nacho.'

'And if *you* were alone here without friends?'

'I can't imagine that,' Grace said, remembering the young girl at the grape-treading and the kindness of Maria and Alejandro.

'You can't imagine being alone in this wilderness?' Nacho pressed.

She huffed a small laugh. 'Wilderness is a state of mind, surely? I've got the same view here as I do in London—that is to say nothing much. But that's okay,' she said, brightening as she thought about it, 'because I like people so much, and I like to think I can make friends anywhere. And don't forget your mother went back for her ring. She must have loved your father or why would she bother? And why would your father try to rescue your mother if he didn't love her?'

'You're such a dreamer, Grace.'

'Is that such a bad thing? Isn't it better to dream happy dreams than have nightmares? Life is fragile, but love is stronger. Sometimes I think we get those two things mixed up. Your parents were human and flawed, but at the end they proved they loved each other. If they were guilty of anything it was taking each other for granted. The real tragedy is that they were killed before they could make things right.'

'And what about us, Grace?'

'Us?'

Biting down on her lip, she looked as if she might cry. Only Grace's sheer force of will drove the tears back, he suspected.

'This is so unfair,' she said, lifting her face to his. 'You're not supposed to read my feelings like a book. I'm supposed to be the one who senses things.'

'So what do your senses tell you, Grace?'

Her eyes welled with tears. 'You make me feel too much,' she said in an angry voice.

'But that's a good thing, isn't it?'

She shook her head, as if he had missed the point entirely. 'Nacho, for goodness' sake, what do you think I am? I would *never* burden you with a blind woman—'

'Stop that.' Dragging Grace into his arms, he embraced her as if his life depended on it, only now realising what he had almost lost. 'Don't you *ever* say anything like that again,' he warned.

'Why not, when it's true?' she said. 'You've spent your life caring for other people. This is *your* time now, Nacho.'

'I'm not going anywhere,' he said, holding Grace tight against his chest. 'Still not,' he said when she made a feeble attempt to push him away.

'I'm warning you—'

'No, you're not,' he argued gently. 'You're asking for reassurance, and that's all I want to give you. I'm not very good at expressing myself, Grace, but in my eyes you're perfect. There's so much I want to show you.' He swore softly beneath his breath, realizing that even now he could get it wrong. 'So much I want you to experience,' he clarified, angry with himself for being so clumsy when words had never mattered more.

This wasn't about Grace being blind, or him wanting to smother or control her. He wanted to protect her when she couldn't help herself, and there were times when even the strongest woman couldn't do that. He wanted to be there for her in the darkness and in the light. He just wanted to be with her—and he wanted Grace to feel the same way about him.

'No, Nacho. I couldn't do that to you.'

She was tempted—God knew she was tempted. There was so much she had grown to love in Argentina—the kindness of the people, the scents and sounds of a new country, the rhythm of life on the vineyard…

And Nacho…

Nacho was a good enough reason as any to go away. She had always prided herself on being a realist, and an affair with Nacho could only leave her shredded and facing a whole new mountain to climb when the affair ended.

Was she a coward now? Too frightened to love?

Love wasn't even a word that was relevant where Nacho was concerned. Her feelings for him were complex. Sexual feelings had mixed with this recent bond of friendship, confusing her into believing what she felt had somewhere to grow. At best they were business associates and maybe friends. And what really frightened her about that was the more he encouraged her the more she might depend on him—losing her freedom, losing her will to fight.

'Grace?'

She turned towards the sound of his voice.

'So you're still with me?' he murmured, in that dark, husky, sexy voice.

'I'm still here,' she confirmed. 'I was just enjoying the sounds of the countryside while I can.'

'You can't wait to leave?'

'My life is in the crowded city. Your life is here on the pampas, with your vineyards and your horses.'

'You sound very sure.'

'I know I can't stay,' she said, determined she wouldn't burden him. Yes, in the light of what had happened today, the truly wonderful news at the vineyard, Nacho was naturally upbeat and could only see bright things in the future—while she liked to think she was more of a realist who knew this burst of light would eventually fade into darkness again.

'You can't stay or you won't?' Nacho demanded.

'I can't *and* I won't,' she said.

Ironically, the birdsong chose the moment Grace decided not to stay with him to reach its climax. The fact that she had refused made no difference to the rowdy and enthusiastic chorus. It was like the wrong soundtrack for a film—discordant and inappropriate.

'So, you won't even stay to celebrate, when people will surely want to thank you for what you've done?'

'It's you they should thank,' she said, wobbling a little as she stood up on the uneven bank. Then she relented. 'I'll stay until I'm sure the vines have recovered—If you want me to.'

'Of course I want you to. What would the celebration be without you? Your prompt action saved the vineyard. I'm going to invite everyone who works here and bring the whole family over to make it something really special for you.'

'I said I'd stay until the vines had recovered. I said nothing about staying on for a party.' She gave a small smile. 'I'm only sorry I won't be here to share it with you.'

'What are you talking about?' Defeat being snatched from the jaws of victory described this moment perfectly. 'What happened to all that brave talk about seeing things through to the end, Grace? You're all right with the bad stuff, but not with the good—is that it?'

'That's not fair,' she protested. 'My job here is done. As soon as I can make a report to Elias with a clear conscience I have to get back to him. You'll get your order,' she said.

His order? He had almost forgotten the damn order.

'I've got to go,' Grace insisted, moving away from him. 'I've got a life to live and a career to pursue.'

'And a duty to see this through!' he shouted after her.

Honouring his promise not to treat Grace as if there was something wrong with her meant watching and doing nothing as she crawled on her hands and knees up the bank, feeling for hazards on the ground along the way. He hated every loathsome second of it—but that was Grace, he accepted. That determined, stubborn, courageous blind woman was who she was, and if he couldn't accept it he should let her go.

He went after her.

'So what's your hurry?' he said. 'What are you so frightened of, Grace?'

'Nothing,' she said, straightening up to confront him, her determined stare missing his face by a mile.

'Then why are you shutting me out?'

'Why am I shutting *you* out? You've got a nerve after the way you've been behaving.'

'Do we need to go back over that?' he demanded, towering over her.

With an angry huff of frustration she felt for a space to get past him, with her arms outstretched like a child about to pin a tail on the donkey. The sight tore him up—but Grace was no child, and the bank was full of potential risk as she climbed rapidly, recklessly, away from him.

'Will you be satisfied when you've fallen into the river?' he demanded in a fury of concern.

She stopped and turned so abruptly he felt sure she'd tumble down the bank. He was aching with tension from standing ready to catch her if she slipped, but even that was nothing to the pain in his heart.

'What are you frightened of, Grace?' he said again.

'Me? Frightened?' she demanded, with an incredulous laugh in her voice.

'*Why* can't you risk giving any part of yourself to another person? *Why* do you always see that as giving up your independence? The Grace who recovered from the challenges you've faced should move on now, not close her mind to possibilities.'

'What possibilities?' she said impatiently. 'I've done everything I've been advised to do. I attended the rehabilitation centre religiously. I learned to read Braille. And thanks to your sister, I have Buddy to help me do practically anything a sighted person can do—'

'I'm talking about personal relationships,' he interrupted. 'What about those, Grace? No one could ever accuse you of falling short where practicalities are concerned.'

'All right!' she exclaimed angrily. 'So you didn't get it the first time. I don't want to be a burden, Nacho. Do you get it now?'

'I'm afraid I don't,' he said. 'Have you considered that it might be you who sees yourself as a burden and no one else does? Can you give me one example of when you've been a burden while you've been here? You have performed better than most experts in your field. And I certainly haven't heard anything to the contrary from my staff. They're very grateful to you, Grace, as I am. So I *don't* get all this nonsense about being a burden.'

Biting down on her lip, she shook her head, as if she couldn't believe he couldn't see the truth in front of his eyes. 'People are wary when they meet me for the first time—like they're not quite sure what I might ask them to do.'

'Stop right there,' he said, grabbing her arms. 'Is that

how Alejandro treated you? Or Maria? Or the old guy at the cantina? Are you saying that's how I am? Or is this all in your head, Grace? Are *you* the one who's guilty of prejudice here? You've had a traumatic time—I get that. And then a healing time of readjustment—I get that too. But now you're on your way, and it's time for you to move forward—not look back. You're so good at helping others. Why can't you help yourself? At least stay on for the party,' he insisted when she started to pull away. 'You helped to avert a catastrophe. You owe yourself that much, Grace.'

'I didn't do it for a pay-off.'

'I'm not saying you did, but you should be gracious enough to allow the people who work here to thank you.'

'Blackmail, Nacho?'

'Whatever it takes,' he said dragging her into his arms.

Nacho's kiss was fierce to begin with, but then it became long and gentle, and after all the passion flying between them what she really wanted now was just for him to hold her so she could stop fighting for a while.

'So what's your answer, Grace? I think I know where you're at,' Nacho added in a whisper against her hair. 'I'm an expert in knowing that when you start a fight it's very hard to draw back and almost impossible to take time out so you can see there could be another, even better way. You don't have to race back to London to find another dragon to slay. Why don't we play out what we've got here and see where it leads?'

'What about my career? I'm just getting started.'

'So go back to London after the celebrations, if that's what you want. I'll just make one more observation. Your knowledge of viticulture is bang up to date, and that's something we're badly in need of here.'

'Are you offering me a job?' she said, lifting her head.

'If you find that suggestion more acceptable than any other,' he said wryly, 'then yes, I am. You've certainly more than proved we need someone like you on the team, Grace.'

'And when my contract ends? This sounds like a short-term contract with long-term repercussions.'

'Why are you always so ready to be hurt? And stop avoiding the issue. Or are you frightened to face the truth?'

'What truth?' she said, frowning.

'That this isn't about the vineyards now. It's about you and me.'

Turning away from him, she hugged herself. 'I don't want to be hurt,' she blurted, burying her chin in her chest. 'I don't think I could handle it.'

'Who says I'm going to hurt you, Grace?' he argued, pulling her close again. 'You've been through a lot—more than I can imagine. Your emotional bank is drained. But you can fill it again and I can help you—if you'll let me.'

'What about Elias and my training? I can't just leave him in the lurch and come and work for you.'

'Can't you do both?' he said. 'I would have thought you could get around the world even faster for Elias with the Acosta jet at your disposal...'

'Are you serious?'

Nacho's answer was to draw her into his arms. 'Never more so,' he said.

Was it wrong to rest here, where she felt so safe? Was it dangerous to admit that together they might be stronger, and that that thought had nothing at all to do with her love of sight?

'You do know Elias is retiring soon?' Nacho said.

'He told you that?' Surprised, she placed her hands flat against his chest, where the beat of Nacho's heart was strong and steady.

'He did more than that,' Nacho explained. Taking her hands, he raised them to his lips, kissing each of them in turn. 'Elias called me and asked if I would be interested in buying his business.'

'What?' she breathed. She was stunned by this new information, but now she could see it made perfect sense for both men. 'Elias could retire in comfort while you would have the whole process covered from vine to glass.'

'An undreamed of advancement for the business,' Nacho confirmed. 'And with you by my side. Come and join me, Grace,' he challenged. 'The vineyards need you, the people who work here need you—I need you.'

'*You* need me?'

Nacho didn't touch her and he didn't speak. This was her decision to make alone. She had never wanted to be a wealthy man's woman, cossetted and protected from the realities of life, and she didn't want it now she was blind. She was used to fighting every day just to stay in the same place. But wasn't fighting for the livelihoods of the people who worked here a battle worth winning too? Wasn't confronting life head-on worth some effort? Or was she going to hide away now she'd reached a certain level in her recovery, and declare herself out?

'Just think of what you could achieve here, Grace— what we could *both* achieve. Don't let your blindness prevent you from taking this next step forward. You've learned to ride while you've been here. What's stopping you now? You can do anything you want to do.'

'What are you saying, Nacho?'

'I'm saying that I love you, and that I want you to stay with me always.'

'You *love* me?'

Terror suffused her. Not at the thought of all the work ahead of her, but at the thought of the biggest step of all... Love. Commitment to love for ever. Committing herself to Nacho. Risking her heart for something bigger than both of them. It was all she wanted, but now she could have it her courage had gone. He was right about her emotional bank being depleted. It was empty. She had nothing left to give him.

'This is where you belong. I belong in London. Please don't fight me on this, Nacho. My decision's made.'

He made no attempt to follow Grace as she struggled to the top of the bank. Her determination was, as ever, uncompromising. When she stumbled she picked herself up. When a tree branch slapped her in the face she pushed it away and moved on. He felt more emotion in those few seconds than he could ever remember feeling before. He had felt little since the day of the tragedy, and nothing came close to this.

But seeing Grace on the point of throwing away her life galvanised him into action, and in a couple of bounds he was ahead of her on the bank. There was only one certainty in his mind. The only woman he had ever loved wasn't going to walk out of his life for ever.

'I won't let you go,' he said fiercely.

'You can't stop me,' she warned, clearly frantic in her darkness.

'You don't have to fight all the time, Grace,' he said, holding her close. 'It's great to be in control—*Dios*, I should know. But it isn't a sign of weakness to share the load. Everyone has to ask for help from time to time, whether they can see or not. Give yourself a break,

Grace. Stand still for a moment and think about what you've accomplished.'

She turned her face towards him and his heart soared.

'Did you really just say you love me?'

'Yes, I did.' Reaching for Grace's hands, he knotted their fingers. 'And I'll never take you for granted,' he whispered fiercely, dragging her into his arms.

Concern for his mistress had brought Buddy snuffling round their feet. 'Not this time, boy,' he murmured as he swept Grace into his arms and carried her towards the cottage. 'I'll take over now...'

He carried Grace up the stairs into the small bedroom, where the windows were open to allow the early evening breeze to cool a room scented with day-warmed frangipani. He undressed her slowly, reverently, and then, stripping off his own clothes, he stretched out beside her on the crisp linen sheets.

'Just hold me,' she whispered.

To hold Grace in his arms was all he wanted. He could think of nothing he wanted more than to sleep with her and wake with her in the morning. To share tomorrow and the next day and the next with Grace. To live with her until they were both old and surrounded by their children and their children's children.

His kisses were slow and easy now, because they had all the time in the world. And when they sighed together, content, at home, complete, he asked her, 'Will you marry me, Grace?'

'I will,' she said, smiling against his mouth.

He felt a great surge of awe and pride that this incredible woman had chosen him. 'I love you,' he murmured after she'd fallen asleep.

'I love you too,' she whispered.

'So you weren't sleeping,' he said, kissing her again.

She nestled her head against his chest. 'You've done so much for me, Grace.'

'I've done so much for *you*?' she queried groggily.

'You've set me free,' he said.

EPILOGUE

ACROSS the world it was dubbed the wedding of the year, but for Grace it was the wedding of a lifetime—her lifetime and Nacho's.

A few carefully screened photographers were to be allowed in to record the event, with all the proceeds going to their new scheme to introduce blind youngsters to horse riding. The marriage ceremony was to be held at the *hacienda*, so it could be a double celebration in which everyone could join in.

It was a real family affair, with Nacho's sister-in-law—the celebrated wedding planner Maxie Acosta—in charge of the arrangements. To ensure Grace enjoyed her day as much as everyone else, Maxie had filled the sumptuously decorated marquee with delicately scented blossoms, and as Grace walked in on the arm of her new husband they crushed rose petals beneath their feet. Elias had been flown in on the family's jet at Nacho's personal invitation, and all the Acostas were there.

Lucia had helped Grace to choose her wedding dress—a dream of filmy silk chiffon, soft to the touch, edged with the finest Swiss lace embellished with tiny crystals and seed pearls because Grace liked the way they tickled her palm and Lucia said she glittered like a queen. There was even a new collar for Buddy, whose new best friend was Cormac, Nacho's Irish Wolfhound. Nacho's big dog had made the trip from the family's main *estancia* in the back of Ruiz Acosta's car.

Grace had only wanted a plain gold wedding band, but a man like Nacho could never be tamed to the extent where Grace would be allowed to instruct him on the subject of the type of jewellery to buy for his wife.

'And thank goodness for it,' Lucia exclaimed after the ceremony, as she examined Grace's diamond-encrusted wedding band. 'You can always have plain gold for everyday.'

Grace laughed indulgently as she hugged her new sister-in-law, glad that some things, like extravagant, fun-loving Lucia, would never change.

'Though I still can't believe Nacho went shopping,' Lucia said, frowning as she held Grace's hand up to the light.

'I think he had the jeweller come to him,' Grace confessed.

'And why not?' a husky voice demanded.

'Talk of the devil,' Lucia murmured dryly, leaving the newlyweds alone.

'I have a very special wedding gift for you,' he murmured, drawing Grace into his arms.

'But you've given me so much already' she said, quivering with love and desire when he found the sweet spot behind her ear.

'Come on,' he prompted, linking his arm through hers.

'Are we going into the *hacienda*?' she said, hearing the gravel path beneath their feet.

'Not for the reason you think,' he said as her breathing

quickened. 'We must be back in time for the first dance, or the wedding breakfast will grind to a halt.'

'But I don't need a gift,' Grace insisted, pulling back. 'I don't need anything but you. I wouldn't be able to see a gift anyway,' she pointed out with her unfailing logic.

'But you'll hear it,' he said. 'Sit…play.' Taking her by the hand, he led her to the piano stool. 'I finally got round to having all the pianos tuned,' he explained. 'They're all yours now, Grace. Everything I have is yours.'

He shouldn't be surprised at the sensitivity in those hands, Nacho realised, but the sounds Grace coaxed from a piano had to be heard to be believed. She made him want to listen to her all night. Well, almost all night, he accepted wryly as his gaze tracked up Grace's arms to the nape of her neck—so soft, so kissable.

'I'm sorry if I'm interrupting—'

He swung round in anger, hearing a woman's voice. Who would dare intrude at a time like this? 'Can I help you?' he asked frostily.

'I've come to take some photographs,' the diminutive photographer informed him boldly.

'Nacho,' Grace murmured, feeling his hackles rise. 'Can *I* help you?' she said, standing up.

'My apologies,' the girl said, speaking to Grace with more respect than she'd shown Nacho. 'I was supposed to check in with someone called Kruz Acosta?'

'My brother isn't here—as you can see,' Nacho cut in with an angry gesture. 'I imagine he's with the other guests in the marquee.'

'Would it be all right to take some photographs now I'm here?' the girl suggested. 'My name's Romily— Romily Winner, from *ROCK!* magazine. The magazine your sister-in-law Holly works for?' she prompted.

'Of course. I've been expecting you. I read your column. It's really good.'

'Thank you.'

'Nacho?' Grace prompted.

'I don't know it,' he said brusquely. 'But if you want some photographs you'd better get on with it. We're needed back at the marquee.'

'Perhaps if Grace could sit at the piano and you could stand behind her?' the girl called Romily suggested.

'Of course we will,' Grace accepted before Nacho could argue.

'So…that was interesting,' Grace said, when Romily had finished the photoshoot and left them. 'Do you think Holly is trying to set your brother up with Romily?'

'Who knows what goes through Holly's head,' he said with a shrug.

'What does she look like?' Grace asked him.

'I wouldn't have thought she was Kruz's type.'

'That's not much help,' Grace said with a laugh in her voice as they walked arm-in-arm to the door.

His lips pressed down as he shook his head, stumped for an answer. 'She looks…alternative.'

'Alternative? Now you *really* have to fill me in.'

'Piercings, tattoos, black eye make-up—leather clothes. As tiny as a whip, but more trouble than any man needs.'

'She sounds interesting,' Grace commented, her lips curving in an amused smile. 'Just what your rebel brother needs.'

'More trouble? I don't think so.' Nacho swung the big oak door wide, but before they stepped outside he brought Grace into his arms and kissed her. 'I suppose we *do* have to get back?' he said.

'To our own wedding breakfast? Yes, I think we must,' Grace said wryly. 'Let's make one condition.'

'Name it,' he said.

'As soon as we've cut the cake you and I come back here alone for dessert.'

'It's a deal,' Nacho agreed, dragging his wife into his arms for a hungry kiss.

* * * * *

#229 SECRETS OF CASTILLO DEL ARCO
Bound by His Ring
Trish Morey
When Gabriella finds herself in alluring Raoul's gothic *castillo,* she knows the key to her lavish prison lies in succumbing to his touch!

#230 MARRIAGE BEHIND THE FACADE
Bound by His Ring
Lynn Raye Harris
It's not easy to divorce a sheikh! Sydney must spend forty nights in the desert—and Sheikh Malik will make sure it's more than worth it....

#231 KEEPING HER UP ALL NIGHT
Temptation on her Doorstep
Anna Cleary
Ex-ballerina Amber knows exactly where noise polluter Guy can put his guitar! But Guy knows a much more exciting use for her sharp tongue!

#232 THE DEVIL AND THE DEEP
Temptation on her Doorstep
Amy Andrews
Forget Johnny Depp...modern-day pirate Rick is pure physical perfection—and just the thing to cure author Stella's writer's block!

REQUEST YOUR FREE BOOKS!

2 FREE NOVELS PLUS
2 FREE GIFTS!

YES! Please send me 2 FREE Harlequin Presents® novels and my 2 FREE gifts (gifts are worth about $10). After receiving them, if I don't wish to receive any more books, I can return the shipping statement marked "cancel." If I don't cancel, I will receive 6 brand-new novels every month and be billed just $4.30 per book in the U.S. or $4.99 per book in Canada. That's a saving of at least 14% off the cover price! It's quite a bargain! Shipping and handling is just 50¢ per book in the U.S. and 75¢ per book in Canada.* I understand that accepting the 2 free books and gifts places me under no obligation to buy anything. I can always return a shipment and cancel at any time. Even if I never buy another book, the two free books and gifts are mine to keep forever.

106/306 HDN FERQ

Name _____
(PLEASE PRINT)

Address _____ Apt. #

City _____ State/Prov. _____ Zip/Postal Code

Signature (if under 18, a parent or guardian must sign)

Mail to the **Reader Service:**
IN U.S.A.: P.O. Box 1867, Buffalo, NY 14240-1867
IN CANADA: P.O. Box 609, Fort Erie, Ontario L2A 5X3

Not valid for current subscribers to Harlequin Presents books.

**Are you a current subscriber to Harlequin Presents books
and want to receive the larger-print edition?
Call 1-800-873-8635 or visit www.ReaderService.com.**

* Terms and prices subject to change without notice. Prices do not include applicable taxes. Sales tax applicable in N.Y. Canadian residents will be charged applicable taxes. Offer not valid in Quebec. This offer is limited to one order per household. All orders subject to credit approval. Credit or debit balances in a customer's account(s) may be offset by any other outstanding balance owed by or to the customer. Please allow 4 to 6 weeks for delivery. Offer available while quantities last.

Your Privacy—The Reader Service is committed to protecting your privacy. Our Privacy Policy is available online at www.ReaderService.com or upon request from the Reader Service.

We make a portion of our mailing list available to reputable third parties that offer products we believe may interest you. If you prefer that we not exchange your name with third parties, or if you wish to clarify or modify your communication preferences, please visit us at www.ReaderService.com/consumerchoice or write to us at Reader Service Preference Service, P.O. Box 9062, Buffalo, NY 14269. Include your complete name and address.

It all starts with a kiss

*Is the Santina-Jackson royal fairy-tale engagement
too good to be true?*

*Read on for a sneak peek of
PLAYING THE ROYAL GAME by* **USA TODAY**
bestselling author Carol Marinelli.

* * *

"I HAVE also spoken to my parents."

"They've heard?"

"They were the ones who alerted me!" Alex said. "We
have aides who monitor the press and the news constantly."
Did she not understand he had been up all night dealing
with this? "I am waiting for the palace to ring—to see how
we will respond."

She couldn't think, her head was spinning in so many
directions and Alex's presence wasn't exactly calming—
not just his tension, not just the impossible situation, but
the sight of him in her kitchen, the memory of his kiss. That
alone would have kept her thoughts occupied for days on
end, but to have to deal with all this, too…. And now the
doorbell was ringing. He followed her as she went to hit the
display button.

"It's my dad." She was actually a bit relieved to see him.
"He'll know what to do, how to handle—"

"I thought you hated scandal," Alex interrupted.

"We'll just say—"

"I don't think you understand." Again he interrupted
her and there was no trace of the man she had met yesterday; instead she faced not the man but the might of

Crown Prince Alessandro Santina. "There is no question that you will go through with this."

"You can't force me." She gave a nervous laugh. "We both know that yesterday was a mistake." She could hear the doorbell ringing. She went to press the intercom but his hand halted her, caught her by the wrist. She shot him the same look she had yesterday, the one that should warn him away, except this morning it did not work.

"You agreed to this, Allegra, the money is sitting in your account." He looked down at the paper. "Of course, we could tell the truth…" He gave a dismissive shrug. "I'm sure they have photos of later."

"It was just a kiss…."

"An expensive kiss," Alex said. "I wonder what the papers would make of it if they found out I bought your services yesterday."

"You wouldn't." She could see it now, could see the horrific headlines—she, Allegra, in the spotlight, but for shameful reasons.

"Oh, Allegra," he said softly but without endearment. "Absolutely I would. It's far too late to change your mind."

* * *

Pick up PLAYING THE ROYAL GAME by Carol Marinelli on November 13, 2012, from Harlequin® Presents®.